BOOKS BY ELIE WIESEL

Night
Dawn
The Accident
The Town Beyond the Wall
The Gates of the Forest
The Jews of Silence
Legends of Our Time
A Beggar in Jerusalem
One Generation After
Souls on Fire
The Oath
Ani Maamin (cantata)
Zalmen, or the Madness of God (play)
Messengers of God
A Jew Today
Four Hasidic Masters
The Trial of God (play)
The Testament
Five Biblical Portraits
Somewhere a Master
The Golem (Illustrated by Mark Podwal)
The Fifth Son

THE
FIFTH
SON

A NOVEL BY

ELIE
WIESEL

TRANSLATED FROM THE FRENCH
BY MARION WIESEL

SUMMIT BOOKS
NEW YORK

Published by SUMMIT BOOKS
A Division of Simon & Schuster, Inc.
Simon & Schuster Building
1230 Avenue of the Americas
New York, New York 10020
Originally published in France as
Le Cinquième Fils by Editions Bernard Grasset
A signed first edition of this book has been
privately printed by The Franklin Library
SUMMIT BOOKS and colophon
are trademarks of Simon & Schuster, Inc.
Manufactured in the United States of America

10   9   8   7   6   5   4   3   2   1

Library of Congress Cataloging in Publication Data

Wiesel, Elie
  The fifth son.

  Translation of: Le cinquième fils.
  I. Title.   II. Title: 5th son.
PQ2683.I32C613   1985   843'.914   84-24071
ISBN 0-671-52331-7

For Elisha
and all the other children of survivors

Blessed is God who gave the Torah to His people Israel, blessed is He. The Torah speaks about four sons: one who is wise and one who is contrary; one who is simple and one who does not even know how to ask a question.

THE PASSOVER HAGGADAH

THE
FIFTH
SON

WAS IT DAWN or dusk? The town of Reshastadt appears crouched and unreal under a steady slow drizzle. Was he already asleep? Or not yet awake? I did not exist for him. I was the bearer of a message, but he was not aware of either message or messenger.

Here is the station. In my confusion, I did not know whether I had just arrived or was preparing to leave again. Was I awake? I was floating in the unreal. Just like the day I followed Lisa on her trip. The same panic oppressed me. The same fist clutched my chest. But that day I loved Lisa—and today I did not love myself.

At one point, inexplicably, I thought I felt my father's presence behind me. I jumped and turned around: "You shouldn't have," he told me as his hand pointed to the station and the streets and the town and the mountains that were already receding. "Forgive me," I stammered. "Forgive me, Father, for having brought you back here, but I had no choice."

My father shook his head unhappily. He was judging me. He was not really here, but his condemnation was real enough. How could I explain it? He hated explanations. He just kept saying: no, no, you shouldn't have.

And so, like long ago, after the trip with Lisa, upon awakening I felt overwhelmed, weighed down with unspeakable remorse; my thoughts confused, my tongue pasty, I felt a stranger to myself.

I began to pace the waiting room. Advertising posters: beautiful girls and their friends their lovers swim and laugh and drink and run and call and offer themselves for little or nothing, for a moment or a lifetime.

I tried to understand myself. I did not succeed. Once on the train, things would be better, that was a promise.

"You shouldn't have," repeats my father. I could reply: "And you?" But I say nothing, I feel guilty. And yet I have done nothing. I feel guilty because I have done nothing.

If only I could get angry, express my rage, but I cannot. . . . And that saddens and annoys me and I resent this insensitive world and my father who understands without understanding that there is nothing to understand, for noise becomes torture and memory drives one mad and the future pushes us back to the edge of the precipice and death envelops us and rocks us and stifles us and, helpless, we can neither cry nor run.

Attention, all passengers. Leaving? Arriving? Goodbye, Reshastadt, the train is arriving, the train arrives, next stop Frankfurt then the airport then the plane then New York and the adventure starts all over again, ecstasy for lovers, prison for beggars, watch out all aboard your ticket *bitte, nicht hinauslehnen, bitte.*

I beg your pardon, Mr. German ticket-taker conductor, I beg your pardon, father, descendant of Abraham, Isaac and Jacob, you are right, I shouldn't have. Why did I go to Germany and why did I seek out this dull and hateful little town? Why renew contact with a past

drowned in blood? To conclude a project which from
the start was doomed to fail? Had I really, truly imagined being able to dominate another man, to crush him,
annihilate him?

I see my father looking at me disapprovingly. Yet it is
his story that has led me here, on this train which seems
to go backward rather than forward. The story of a
man who survived by chance and, by chance, rediscovered his wife and her demons. The story of a leader
who, again by chance, was called upon to play a role he
never really wanted.

Poor father. He thought he was strong, stronger than
the enemy. My turn to tell him: "You shouldn't
have. . . ." Were he here, I would rest my head on his
shoulder. Were he here, I would break down and weep.

I know: the things I say about my father disconcert
you; what I am about to say will perhaps disconcert you
further. Am I old-fashioned? I love my father. I love
him down to his weaknesses. When we are apart, all I
have to do is think of him and everything around me,
everything inside me becomes transparent. Words burst
into flames and roar until I shut my ears. My father's
voice reaches me from another world. I feel excluded,
rejected.

Of course, we have had our differences which at
times turned into bitter arguments; then I would bite
my lip so as not to cry out. That is natural, human: love
is a series of scars. "No heart is as whole as a broken
heart," said the celebrated Rabbi Nahman of Bratzlav.
My father broke my heart more than once; even now, as
I speak of it, I hurt.

For he affects me, my father does. Nobody has ever
affected me as deeply. There are times when I think of

him, grave and unsmiling, and tears well up in my eyes. I feel both caught and liberated by a force that comes from far away. His every word, his every glance is for me a place, a moment of fusion. Every contact with him becomes reflection and encounter. Two exiles are joined in a single exhortation.

Yet there is nothing extraordinary about his appearance. He is an average man, of average height, with an average income, living in an average house in a neighborhood for average residents. A refugee like so many others in a city whose ethnic pluralism is its true pride. Except for the fact that he shows no interest in baseball and football, he follows the rules of the "American way of life." Vitamins, ready-made clothes and *The New York Times*. Neither his way of speaking nor his manner of keeping silent attracts attention. He seeks anonymity. One must see him at close range to take notice. But then one cannot turn away. His eyes, his beautiful grave eyes, peer out from under heavy lids and bring you under their spell. If you are sensitive to the human face, you will not be able to free yourself of his; it suggests a distant darkness. But my father shuns observation. Eyes are cumbersome, he says, intrusive. Surely that is not the real reason. The real reason, in my opinion, has to do with the war. During that time, in Europe, one had to lose oneself in the crowd, melt into the night. To survive, one needed not to exist.

One day, much later, somewhere in the Orient, a sage studied the lines of my hand and face, considered my destiny and shook his head, signifying great confusion: "Your case, my young traveler, leaves me perplexed: this is the first time it happens to me. I situate you within the flow of time and within the memory that restrains time. I see you kneeling before the gods of knowledge and the goddesses of passion. I see you standing before their priests. I recognize you among your friends, I discover you face-to-face with your enemies. But one being is missing from the landscape; I do not see your father." A troubled light then appeared in his dark eyes. And he added, softly: "Help me, yes, help me rediscover your father."

For he has mastered the art of leaving, my father. You speak to him, he seems to listen to you, but suddenly, in the middle of a sentence, you sense his disappearance. In the subway, during rush hour, people jostle him but they do not see him. Whether out of excessive discretion or shyness, he is afraid to disturb, to exert a harmful influence, to provoke disasters, who knows, perhaps even earthquakes.

He is a loner, my father. He feels at ease only among dead or invented characters who, locked into or liberated in thousands upon thousands of volumes, live in his imagination. Being a librarian, he chats with Homer and Saul, Jeremiah and Virgil. A passionate reader, he never goes anywhere without a book under his arm. At home as in the office, on the bus or in the park, he is forever "beginning" or "finishing" a study, a commentary by so-and-so on so-and-so or against so-and-so.

We live in Brooklyn surrounded by Hasidim. For them, life is one continuous song. That is all right with me but their non-Jewish neighbors must not be too pleased with it all. Do these Hasidim ever sleep? Of course, you see, it is quite possible that they sing even in their sleep. Which would explain why their sad songs are so joyous and why their joyous songs are so sad. No, it would not explain anything, too bad.

As for my father, he loves them. He reads their pamphlets, which he buys by the dozen. As soon as he comes home, he spreads them out on the table in the living room, or the one in the kitchen, and he begins to read them fast, very fast, as though he were dreading a catastrophe that would make them disappear. Have I mentioned the bleak light reflected in his eyes as he reads? He looks as if he is in pain, so intense is the joy he derives from reading.

Before, I mean: before my mother's departure, before her sickness, he would spend hours in the semidarkness of his library where books were piled helter-skelter, on makeshift bookshelves and on the floor. These days, he likes to settle down in the living room to read. Since the light bothers him, he unscrewed three bulbs from the tarnished chandelier. Strange, the semidarkness accompanies him and envelops him like a ritual shawl. When I see him like that, cut off from the world, so vulnerable in his isolation, I feel like sneaking up on him, hugging and comforting him; I feel like offering him my youth and my yearning for sunshine. Fortunately, my reticence always prevails and I withdraw.

So as not to embarrass me, he pretends not to have seen anything. But I am not deceived. I know that he sees everything, that he is aware of everything, that nothing escapes him.

What interests him? I don't know. Sometimes he seems profoundly indifferent to life's sounds. Did I say indifferent? Rather: inaccessible. . . . Absent. . . . No, I must correct myself once more: elsewhere . . .

Elsewhere? I know the place. I think I know it. Or at least I can imagine it. It is a strange and real kingdom, a strangely real kingdom, one in which values are reversed, dreams are violent, laughter is delirious and silent. It is a kingdom in which one is forever dying, forever keeping silent, for the storm that blows there is a storm of ashes.

My father lived there. So did my mother. How did they manage to survive? I do not know, neither do they. Absolute Evil was opposed by a Good that was only theoretical, therein lay the tragedy. "You won't understand," whispered my father. "Nobody will understand." And my mother, in the very beginning, would agree: "As for me, it is God I do not understand." To which my father answered: "And who tells you that God Himself understands?"

I should so like him to open his memory to mine. I would give all I possess to be able to follow him on his obscure paths. Let him speak and I shall listen with my entire being and never mind if I ache for him, for us. . . . But he does not speak. He does not want to speak. Perhaps he cannot. . . .

When he condescends to speak to me, it frequently is to discuss his favorite author, One-Eyed Paritus, whose *Oblique Meditations* influenced the religious and antireligious ideas of more than one medieval philosopher. As he quotes from him, he strokes his forehead and cheeks, he becomes thoughtful, kind, beautiful. All at once, I too came to love Paritus, for he was giving me back my father.

As a child and adolescent I could not do without his presence, his sadness. Every evening, between school and bedtime, I followed him step-by-step, I tracked him in his memories, his walled-in visions. One day, he said, I would visit his native town, I would appear in Davarowsk between Kolomey and Kamenetz-Bokrotay, in the shadow of the Carpathian Mountains, and I would admire the sky that witnessed his birth and the fences he surely climbed and the trees whose fruit he picked; I would inhale the smoke of the chimneys and the smell of the fields; I would gaze at the silvery reflection of the river, the shuttered windows of the asylums echoing endless laments. Oh yes, one day I would wake up in the ghost town of Davarowsk and I would call out: "Father, come and look, you are no longer the only one who haunts this cursed town with its cursed fate, I am with you, we won!"

It would not be easy. For my father is cautious. He proceeds only on sure ground, always alone. Forbidden to knock at his door. He says only whatever he feels like saying, or else he says one thing to conceal another. Impossible to provoke him, to rush him. At the first sign of misplaced curiosity he erects his barriers.

Of course, there were times when I was resentful. It hurt me to see, to know that he was alone in his struggle against invisible assailants. I was dying to fly to his rescue, to fight at his side. I would raise my voice, demand an explanation. All I did was increase his pain.

I remember: being a student of philosophy, preoccupied with problems of suffering, my head bursting with Buddhism, Schopenhauer, the Ecclesiastes, I would turn my knowledge, my semblance of knowledge, against him. I remember: one winter evening, I was feeling particularly low, pining for Lisa. (I shall talk about her later); I took it out on him and reproached him his suffering:

"Don't you understand that to accept suffering is evil and dangerous? It is like choosing nothingness over being. . . . Fate over oneself."

He did not seem surprised, only sad. He pretended to finish the sentence he was reading, then raised his eyes and gazed at me: it was the gaze of a living man, a serious, dignified, austere consciousness; a gaze turned inward, a consciousness thoroughly cognizant of itself.

Then the gaze went dark and the world went dark and
I told myself: this is where the mystery begins.

I also told myself: this is how he is. Nothing I can do
about it. Out of reach. I shall have to wait some more.
Respect his freedom. Like everyone, he is free to do as
he pleases with his past. Free to be a prisoner or sover-
eign, resigned or rebellious, friend of the dead or ally of
the living. Free to renounce his freedom. I had better
accept that.

Not that he shuns society, but he does distrust it. One
never knows: outsiders may look where they should not.
For instance, when I was a child I was taken to school
by my mother, when I really wanted my father to take
me there. The other children made fun of me: "What
about your father, hmm? Ashamed to show himself?"
"My father," I would answer, "has no time for this; he
is too busy. He has better things to do."

One day, my mother baked a chocolate cake; it must
have been my fourth or fifth birthday. After dinner, she
cut the cake and sighed: "We should have invited his
little friends." Whereupon my father totally withdrew
into himself. He became scowling, hostile. I did not understand: I had done nothing wrong, neither had my
mother. We left the table without a word and without
touching the cake. Since then, nobody has ever celebrated my birthday. "Don't be sad," said my mother.
"Your father does not like strangers: he likes only his
own." A satisfactory but incomplete explanation. There
was another reason. A secret one. My father was afraid
of children; they frightened him and brought back his
old fear. And so did I.

M*y dear son,*

Since I tell you everything, surely you know that I belong to an extinct race, an extinct species; I have invoked every name, exposed every face of the crepuscular beast and yet I have not shortened mankind's wait.

There was a time when I knew the goal but not the road; now it is the opposite. Perhaps not even that. There is more than one path open to us. Which one leads toward God, which one leads toward man? I am just a wanderer. Still I go on searching. Perhaps all I seek is to remain that wanderer.

I have nothing left but words, outdated words, useless beneath their multiple disguises, scattered over the cemeteries of the exiled. I let myself be guided by them because I seek to comprehend the essence of things, the Being beyond beings.

How long shall I remain a prisoner? Don't leave me, my son.

Your father

Dear son,

Your mother is sick and I despair. Incurable, say the doctors. She will not get up again. I imagine Job's wife without Job and it is your mother I see.

With you, she was still playing these last weeks; she will not play again.

How long has she been like this, dead among the living, believing herself dead among the dead?

Difficult to establish, answer the specialists. But I know: a long time. Since the ghetto. I mean to say: since that night in the ghetto, since the night of the separation. That is the appropriate word for it, my son: a separation between beings, words, moments.

Nothing was going right: that is what we thought in the ghetto. All the calculations were wrong. The forecasts, the illusions, the assurances: a cosmic error had insinuated itself into the crevices of life and mind.

That night, in an act of primal uprooting, your mother broke with all of us, and with herself.

We did not realize it until later.

Now.

Is she at least closer to you?

Your father

My son,

Do you know that I am looking at you? I would so like to listen to you, but you are silent. Are you afraid to break the silence? Are you afraid to speak to me? Afraid to frighten me? But, son,

*nothing frightens me anymore. Even death only oppresses me. I
look at it and I am glad that it is mute. What would I do if it
began to speak to me, to speak to me of you?*

*I look at you, my son, my gaze is seeking yours. Your eyes
make mine sparkle, your eyes glow in mine. What do they see? A
limited, impoverished future? A sullied, desecrated eternity?
Speak and I too shall speak.*

*Of the two of us, you are the one who has the right to say any-
thing. You have measured the frailty of so-called immutable
laws, you have plumbed the depths of the abyss. You have seen
and endured man's truth. Have you seen God, tell me?*

*I think of you, my son, and I am troubled: my knowledge comes
between us as a wedge. It keeps me alive and relegates you to the
distance. A private insight into the future? You are my future, my
son. "And mine?" you might well ask me. But you ask nothing.
Your silence both drives me away and attracts me and I seek refuge near my Master whose philosophy would surely amuse you.*

*As for me, I recognize the value of meditation suspended in
time; to meditate on something is to renew it. Only I am afraid, I
write to you and I am afraid. I speak to you and I am afraid. In
me, nothing but fear renews itself.*

Your father

My son,

*Can you explain the mystery of death to me? It is as difficult to
understand as the mystery of survival.*

*Why me? Why your mother? Our parents must have entrusted
us with a message when they left us: I should like to retrieve it.
Or at least locate it. Make it mine. Make it me.*

*I am speaking to you, my son, in order to convince myself that
I am still capable of speech. The silence within me at times be-*

comes so heavy that my heart comes close to bursting. But the fact is: I don't want to part with this silence. I am searching for a special course: one that lies between words and silence. As I am searching for a special time: one that lies between life and death. No, let me correct myself: between the living and the dead.

I am searching for you, my son.

But I have never done anything but search for you. I search for you in the void that rejects me. I search for myself in you whom I have, however unwillingly, abandoned.

Your father

M Y MOTHER, yes, my mother. What can I say? My poor unhappy mother. He is awaiting her recovery, her return to society, to life, while knowing all the while that her prison is of a special kind: the kind one never leaves.

I think of my mother often, yet I never speak of her for fear of hurting my father: why reopen his wounds?

I was six at the time of our separation. I remember: the white-coated doctor, the efficient orderlies, the ambulance, the stretcher; the neighbors in the street whispering about the drama, the tragedy of that poor Rachel Tamiroff who ... And my father, pale, his lips white and trembling, his gaze that of a beaten and humiliated man. And my poor mother complaining that something was lacking, lacking: "What is it you are lacking?" the physician is asking her. "Is it air? Money?" She does not hear him. While the orderlies bustle about the room, she goes on whispering that she is missing something, something. ... As for me, overwhelmed with pain and also with shame, I sit in my corner and watch, I become my own gaze, I feel that my gaze is torn from its source and is leaving me just as my mother is leaving me. . . .

And now she is gone, my mother. Without my having had a chance to tell her that simple, unequivocal truth: that her solemn beauty upset me, that her anguish tore me apart, that her delicate fingers, her long eyelashes drew me toward her as to a shadowy shore. Did she know, does she know, that I needed to see her fine, impassive face to defeat the demons that lay in ambush? Yes, my mother allowed herself to be carried away without my having had a chance to confess my love to her.

Never will she know the tenderness or the violence she inspired in me. True I was small but I knew how to love and my memory is good.

Leaning against the table in the big living room, her back to the window overlooking the noisy avenue, she proved to be astonishingly clever at repairing a torn piece of clothing, a twisted candlestick, a broken watch. She knew how to concentrate on whatever she was doing, except that sometimes, abruptly, as though struck by an invisible whip, she would freeze. And then, a shiver would run down my spine.

Yet I loved to watch her. Unbeknownst to her, from afar, troubled, tense, I would look at her hands, stare at her throat. At times she would smile and my heart would turn cold. Who was she smiling at?

Whenever I spoke to her I blushed. The fear of giving myself away made me clumsy, incoherent. I pursued and fled her foolishly. She intimidated me and, strangely, I seemed to intimidate her too, though I was just her five- or six-year-old boy. Like criminals we would turn away the moment our eyes met. To show me her affection, to demonstrate my love to her, we each needed a pretext, an alibi. She kissed me only when I was sick. Since she left, I have rarely been sick.

Now it is she who is sick. I do not know the cause of the illness that is draining her. I only know that she is in treatment, that she is allowed almost no visitors, that the physicians are pessimistic—oh, I know a great deal about that: I know that I am living her years as well; I feel them being added to mine; my father knows it too but we have both chosen not to speak of it.

Why? Out of simple respect for her? For fear of aggravating her condition? I have a vague feeling that my father's silence is not unrelated to me. I may be wrong, I may be exaggerating; I may be inventing my faults so as to punish myself and thus participate in his torture from afar. In any case, one day I asked my father the question:

"Her illness, when did it start?"

"Not today and not yesterday," he replied.

And, after a moment of awkwardness, he went back to the *Meditations* of his beloved Paritus. I had the impertinence to insist:

"Forgive me, Father, but couldn't you be more specific?"

When, finally, his eyes came to rest on me, I read in them so many tormented thoughts that I understood: it was better to acquiesce.

Still, I do remember an incident which, though undoubtedly insignificant, could, after all, provide a small clue: my mother looks at me but does not see me; she does not see me but she speaks to me. It seems strange but that is how it was; the image is clear in my mind.

It is Friday evening. Father is in the House of Study next door. He will be home soon. The living room: welcoming, bright, the whiteness of *Shabbat* . . . the majesty

of *Shabbat* . . . and, above all, the peace of *Shabbat.* . . .
My mother, who has recited the blessing over the candles, sits down and stares at the small flickering flames.
Overcome by a new emotion, I dare not move. I lean
against the wall, I admire my mother's hair, my
mother's dress. Deep inside me I *know* that her beauty,
her serenity, spring from her love, from her love for me.
And so I take one step forward and another, I sit down
at her right, I place my arm on hers, I want her to look
at me. She looks at me, she speaks to me, she uses words
that should make me happy; they are so gentle and
tender; but they evoke in me a nameless sadness, for I
know, I feel that she does not see me. . . .

I am about to burst into tears when the door opens
and my father appears: "Good Shabbos," he greets us
with the smile he reserves for *Shabbat.* We do not answer. His expression changes when he sees my mother
who is still speaking to the flickering candles. "Go into
your room," he whispers to me. "I must be alone with
your mother a moment." He comes for me an hour
later. During the meal, I observe my mother. She no
longer looks at the candles. But neither does she look at
us. She looks at nothing. From that moment on, her
gaze is empty.

Must I say how saddened I was by her "departure"?
Is it really necessary? I found myself roaming from
room to room in the apartment like some fugitive,
jumping from activity to activity, hovering in corners,
seeking refuge under the table, never allowing my father to leave me. I followed him like a shadow, to the
library, to the supermarket, to the House of Study. I
helped him do the housework, rearrange the books on
the shelves. I was panic-stricken at the idea of remaining alone, abandoned.

To make things worse, my mother's "departure" coincided with the Passover holiday. Brooklyn welcoming spring is like an orchestra tuning its instruments. Everything is moving, changing, the street is but one long resounding laugh. Not this time. Not for me. No sooner was I outside than I would begin to anxiously pull at my father's sleeve: "Let's go home quickly. *Someone* may be waiting for us. . . ."

I shall never forget that Passover. Together, my father and I had bought the wine and the traditional foods. We had refused our neighbor's invitation, having decided to celebrate the *Seder* at home. Inside me a small obstinate voice said: "She will come back and won't find us." And then too, like every year, for every holiday, Simha-the-Dark, my father's friend, had joined us to share our solemn repast.

Before blessing the wine, my father looked me straight in the eyes and placed his hands on my shoulders:

"The Law orders us to celebrate this holiday with joy," he said. "Make an effort."

"And . . . Mommy?"

"Do it for her."

"But . . . what about her? What is she doing right now? Promise me that she too will be joyous during the coming week."

My father took a deep breath but said nothing. Simha-the-Dark spoke for him:

"Your mother is a good Jew, she knows the laws; she knows that we have no right to hide from joy."

"I don't understand," I said through my tears.

"Never mind," said Simha-the-Dark. "The Law does not require us to understand, only to live in joy."

"I still don't understand."

"Imagine," said Simha-the-Dark, "imagine a joy

that, for almost four thousand years, is waiting for you to be received; without you, it would roam like an orphan in search of a home."

"I cannot imagine. As soon as I begin to imagine, I see Mommy, I see nothing but her."

"Let us say *Kiddush,*" said my father, beginning the prayers. Then came my turn to ask the traditional four questions: In what way is this Passover night different from any other night of the year? In the book of the *Haggadah,* my father read the response: For we were slaves, long ago, in Egypt. But that was not the real answer. I knew the real answer: this night was different because my mother was in exile, far away. And Simha, Simha-the-Dark, nodded his agreement.

"Yes, you are right. Your mother is in exile. Just like the *Shekhina* who is also in exile. That is why your joy is not complete and neither is ours. And neither is the Lord's."

According to tradition, Father was to narrate the Exodus of our people toward freedom, but Simha chose to tell me another story first:

"The *Shekhina* is a beautiful and sad woman crowned with a halo of shadow and light. One meets her at midnight wherever Jewish children call her to heal the sick and console the wretched. One day a Roman officer glimpsed her hovering over the ruins of Jerusalem. Dazzled by her somber beauty, he fell in love. He moved toward her but could not reach her. It was as though he were treading water; all he could do was look at her from afar. It broke his heart. Then and only then did she smile at him. And because of that smile he remained in Jerusalem till the end of his life. To his friends he explained: since the woman cannot be mine, I shall content myself with her shadow."

When Simha expounds on his favorite subject, he ac-

cedes to the sublime; I would gladly listen to him from
morning till night. As he speaks, his eyes light up and
shine with a special, disquieting brilliance. His delivery
is slow and spellbinding; he discards the words as if they
were green fruit; but he strokes and warms them before
he parts with them.

"Do you know the story of the great Rabbi Haim-
Gedalia of Ushpitzin?" he asks me another evening.
"He interceded with God in favor of an innkeeper who
was notorious for his many sins. 'Very well, I forgive
him,' said the Almighty. Whereupon, pleased with his
success, the Rabbi began to look for sinners to defend in
heaven. Only this time he could not make himself
heard. Overcome with remorse, the Rabbi fasted six
times six days and asked heaven the reason for his dis-
grace. 'You were wrong to look for sinners,' a celestial
voice told him. 'If God chooses to look away, you should
do the same.' And the Rabbi understood that some
things must remain in the shadows, for the shadows too
are given by God."

Dear Simha. Does he really think that I believe his
shadow stories? I am no longer a child, but in his presence I become one. Even today I feel like a very small
boy when he speaks to me or when he listens to me.
With my father, it is different. With my father I sometimes feel old, very old, don't laugh: I feel older than he.

And as resigned.

Like now, in this German station, on this German
train. I call on him to be my witness and speak to him
almost as his peer:

"I am like you after all. As incompetent as you, and
as ineffective. My head in the clouds. Incapable of ac-
complishing a mission. Incapable of endowing the deed

with a redeeming purpose. Don't tell me I should not
have come, I know that. Haven't you ever done things
you shouldn't have? Haven't you ever made journeys
that led nowhere? Haven't you followed this same road,
Father? Admit it, admit without fear or shame that we
have failed together. Together we shall taste defeat."

The train is picking up speed. Sounds of windows
being slammed, doors being opened, fugitives being
shot: it is a flight, a flight from slavery, a race toward
freedom. Suddenly I forget the train, I see myself running side by side with my father, breathless, terrified, I
question him: Mother where is Mother I want to know I
must know but I shall know nothing. Another change of
scene: Passover eve we are recounting, chanting, the
ancient tale of our ancestors' departure, a wild, exhil-
arating race, I am looking for Moses and Moses is looking for us and the Egyptian soldiers are hounding us,
driving us into the sea and they are following us into
the sea and it is victory and like the angels I love to sing
and like the angels I am reprimanded by God one does
not sing in the presence of death one does not sing of
death and I say to God thank you thank you Lord for
having killed our enemies thank you for having killed
them yourself thank you for having spared us that task
and God answers one does not say thank you in the
presence of death one does not say thank you to death.

But then, Father, when does one say thank you? And
to whom?

I REMEMBER another Passover. Once more there were two of us reciting the *Haggadah.* Simha-the-Dark for once was silent. Suddenly he interrupted us:

"Reuven," he said to my father, "fulfill your duty as a Jewish father."

My father looked at him perplexed but did not answer.

"The *Haggadah,*" continued Simha, "tells us of the four sons and their attitude toward *the question.* The first knows the question and assumes it; the second knows the question and rejects it; the third endures the question with indifference; the fourth does not even know the question. There is, of course, a fifth son, but he does not appear in the tale because he is gone. Thus, the duty of a Jewish father is to the living. When will you finally understand, Reuven, that the dead are not part of the *Haggadah?*"

"And you," said my father with a forced smile, "when will your ears finally hear what your mouth is saying?"

"It's different for me," said Simha. "Hanna lives in my thoughts, but she does not dominate them. And

35

then too, Reuven, you know it well: I am not anybody's
father."

My father looked up at him briefly and without answering, continued the reading of the prayers and
poems as though he had never been interrupted.

After the meal, he turned to his friend and said:

"You may be right."

And to me:

"I'd like to tell you something of my youth. . . .

"In the beginning, I was like the first son. Faithful to
Jewish tradition, I obeyed its laws with fervor. I had
but one desire: to resemble my father, a simple, upright
man, a man of flawless integrity. Then came the demon
who seduced me: like the second son, I rebelled against
our people. Like him, I said: your history does not concern me. Like him, I listened to the Egyptian prince
who, in James Joyce's *Ulysses,* beseeches Moses not to
renounce his luxurious way of life, the grandiose adventures and the civilization that the Pharaoh's kingdom reserved for its intelligent and privileged citizens.
Whatever would he do with this poor tribe in the immense and deadly desert? A logical and convincing argument that Moses had the courage to reject; not I, I
found it attractive. That's the truth, my son: the Jews
left Egypt but I chose not to follow them. Instead I followed a friend who had left our village to continue his
studies in Davarowsk.

"I was fascinated by that friend. His original and
blasphemous theories succeeded in demolishing everything while attempting to explain everything. His
theories propounded not only the right but the duty of
Jews to repudiate their ancestral bonds, to assimilate,
to forget their heritage. To forget so as to be able to be-

come assimilated, that was his motto. He observed none
of the commandments, bowed to no interdiction, celebrated no holiday. As far as he was concerned, Napo-
leon and Kant had dethroned Moses and Joshua: down
with religious dogma, long live emancipation. A prag-
matist and opportunist, he had himself baptized and
tried to convince me to do the same. A young missionary had persuaded him. With me, they failed. The
image of my parents protected me: there was a limit to
the humiliation, the pain I could inflict on them. I de-
fined myself as an agnostic. Hoping still to win me over
and convert me, the young missionary arranged for my
admission to the University of Davarowsk. There, I immersed myself in the study of the classics. I discovered
One-Eyed Paritus to whom I devoted myself body and
soul and soon they were predicting a brilliant academic
career for me. My essay on Paritus made a splash in the
capital; it was widely discussed in the press.

"The Jewish community prided itself on the fact that
I had refused to be baptized. People talked about me in
shops, restaurants, Talmudic schools: if only I could be
brought back into the fold! Eloquent and not so eloquent emissaries were dispatched to me. Some spoke to
me of theology, others of politics. Some even offered me
large sums of money. Or their daughters in marriage.
Vain attempts. Courteously but firmly, I bade them all
farewell without even bothering to explain to them the
absurdity of their undertaking.

"That is when Rabbi Aharon-Asher, grandson of the
great preacher bearing the same name, invited me to
come and see him: never had anyone been known to
decline such a great honor. My refusal established a
precedent which, as you can imagine, aroused general
indignation. The butchers declared themselves willing
and able to teach me a lesson; the carpenters agreed but

suggested waiting until nightfall. Had it not been for the Rabbi's intervention, I would have been treated to a nasty beating. Instead, accompanied by his assistant, he took the trouble to come and knock at my door. I did not realize then that by coming he had saved my life; even so, his action embarrassed me:

" 'I must speak to you, Reuven Tamiroff. May I come in?'

"I led him into my study and motioned him to a chair:

" 'Please sit down, you'll be comfortable there!'

" 'Nonsense! Who wants to be comfortable!'

"He stood, towering over me by a full head.

" 'I am listening,' I said.

"The Rabbi was in his forties, heavyset, with an energetic face and a sharp gaze. He was authority incarnate. When he spoke one listened. Precise, irrefutable thoughts. Short, clipped sentences.

" 'It seems,' he said, 'that you persist in cutting yourself off from the community. Why?'

" 'I don't know.'

"It was not a lie. I could not have lied in his presence. I had simply forgotten the arguments my converted friend had used in snaring me.

" 'You must have listened to alien voices,' said the Rabbi. 'Why don't you listen to your own? The memory I live with is not different from yours; the words that rush to my lips you could utter and just as well! Why do you seek to turn your back on yourself? Don't give me excuses or alibis! Don't tell me that it is easier, more comfortable! It is not, and you know it. For a Jew like yourself, it is more complicated, more cumbersome, more dangerous. . . . Do you know the anecdote of the Talmudic sage and the fish? At the time of the Roman persecutions, the governor of Judaea advised a Jewish

sage to give up the Torah in order to survive. To which
the sage responded with the following parable: "One
day, the fox spoke to the fish and gave them this advice:— Look, you all fear the fishermen and their nets,
why don't you leave the sea for dry land? — How foolish you are, answered the fish; our only chance of survival is in the water. . . . It is the same for the Torah,"
added the sage. And it is the same for you, Reuven Tamiroff. Your only chance of survival lies within the
community; it needs you . . . you need it.'

"He paused, out of breath, and moved his heavy
head closer to mine with a movement I perceived as
violent, devastating. I had hardly spoken and yet I too
felt breathless.

" 'I am afraid,' I said almost reluctantly, 'I am afraid
of the fishermen.'

" 'Then come back! Cling to me, to us, I shall help
you! I shall help you defeat Death and even the fear of
Death!'

"He was launched, Rabbi Aharon-Asher, grandson
of the great preacher of the same name, and there was
no stopping him. He continued without a pause, quoting from Scriptures and evoking prophetic visions,
Abraham's trial and the sacrifice of Isaac, the Talmud
and its Masters, their common sufferings, their agony,
our ordeals and lamentations during the course of centuries. As though reluctant to stop for fear of losing his
powers, he spoke for an hour or two, perhaps even
longer:

" 'Of course Death loves to ravage our ranks, of
course we have endured too many persecutions in too
many nations and for too many reasons, but what does
that mean? It means that we live in spite of Death, that
we survive Death! It means that our history, our prodi-
gious history, is a permanent challenge to reason and

fanaticism, to the executioners and their power! Would you really want to desert such a history?'

"I don't know who won that day. I only know that I nodded several times: yes, I understood; yes, I was aware of the deeper meaning of Jewish tradition, but . . . I made no promises, no commitments. It was not in my nature to act impulsively. I wanted to think, analyze, explore all options.

"Having said this, I must admit: if I did not remain the second son of the *Haggadah,* it is thanks to my master and friend, the grandson of the great preacher Rabbi Aharon-Asher."

My father fell silent. The candlelight illuminated his lined, angular face. Shaken, I did not say a word. This was the first time he had spoken to me of his former life. I was about to thank him but Simha spoke first:

"What about the *fifth son,* Reuven? When will you tell him about the *fifth son?*"

His face ashen, my father bowed his head as though overcome by a remorse he dared not put into words.

M*y son,*

That evening, you came to tell me . . . [illegible] . . . *The words you pronounced were sad, but the way you said them made me smile.*

I like it when you make me smile.

Your father

Dear son,

Your presence is essential to me. It is an integral part of me; I sense it in my sleep, I rediscover it when I open my eyes. And yet. You know what life has made of all of us.

The last Passover in the ghetto. . . . *It erupts suddenly into my consciousness, I wonder why. All those guests at the table. Faces, familiar and strange. Songs of joy mixed with anguish. Simha intones a most beautiful and solemn song: "Forever and everywhere, enemies rise, threatening to annihilate us, but forever*

*and everywhere, the Lord, blessed-be-He, comes to our rescue."
We sing with him. Your mother is clenching her teeth, holding
back her tears. I tell her: "Look, look at your son and your sadness will go away." But when she does look at you she bursts
into tears. And so I say to her . . . [illegible] . . .
I was proud of you that evening, my son.
   I still am today.*

Your father

*P.S. I think of Simha's song. Is it true that God always inter-
venes? Did he save our generation? He saved me. Is that reason
enough for me to tell Him of my gratitude?*

I HAD TO COME to Germany, to this small gray town, to pierce the mystery that separated me from my father. I look at myself in this place and I understand at last. Like him, I do not wish to speak; like him, I am wary.

Come to think of it, he was wary of me. Why? What had I ever done to him? How had I displeased him? I said it earlier; he rarely reached out, spoke little, hardly at all, that is to say, in spurts, in unpredictable and disconcerting ways, and then only of current events and trivia: "Did you read in the paper that . . . ? You won't forget to . . . ?" Sometimes, when I urged him on, he would offer me a crumb from his childhood, a scrap from his adolescence, an episode from his student days. But as soon as we broached the forbidden topic of war, he would clear his throat and appear frightened and intensely weary: it's late, he would say. Time to go to sleep. To eat. To go into the city for a lecture. To prepare a suddenly urgent file. And then, it was pointless to insist. He became withdrawn. Distant. Visibly overcome by a great sadness, an unspeakable anguish from long ago. I would give up immediately and change the subject, but vow to try again.

Now I know what frightened him. I know that he felt guilty. And I also know that he was wrong. Who do I know this from? From myself, that's who. From myself, his son. For we resemble one another. I carry within me his past and his secret. The ancient sages were right: everything is contained in the I and it is myself I question in order to understand my father.

Only once did he speak to me seriously, I mean at length, directly, man to man, like two adults, two partners: on the eve of my *Bar Mitzva*. It was to be celebrated the following day, during *Shabbat* services, in a Hasidic House of Study of which we were, though unofficially, members in good standing. Other immigrants and refugees from Davarowsk also attended services there. As for the rabbi, he was the nephew of Rabbi Aharon-Asher of Davarowsk.

The arrival of a new member into the community is a joyous and solemn event. Adolescent in the morning, adult in the evening, the boy quickly becomes aware of the duties that bind him to the collective fate of Israel. To encourage him, to congratulate him, to make his star shine in the blue sky of a people intoxicated with God and eternity, the community sings for him and drinks with him. But neither my father nor I was in the mood for drinking or singing. I was thinking of my poor mother and I felt my eyes growing heavy. . . .

"Are you ready?" my father asked me.

Of course I was, as much as any boy my age could be. Ready for the ceremony. Ready for the stages ahead.

"The blessings?"

"I know them by heart."

I had studied the sacred texts and various commentaries at the *Yeshiva* and I had also learned the melodies of the Biblical readings and the prophetic *Haftara.*

"Did you prepare a speech?"

"No."

"Long ago, in the old country, boys would seize this opportunity to expound a *Khidush,* an original idea, a striking concept linked to a Talmudic theme. The object was for the disciple to prove to his masters that their faith in him was justified."

"Not in America," I said. "You know perfectly well, Father: in America the ceremony is incidental; what counts is the festivity. The eating. The drinking."

To be honest I had another reason for not wanting to make a speech: I was afraid that I might lose control, burst into tears. My father understood. He tried to smile:

"Do you know what the great Rabbi Mendel of Kotzk said? The most beautiful speech is the speech one does not pronounce."

And so, on this particular Friday night, standing before the three lighted candles, I felt more oppressed than usual. In my mind I was drawing up my balance sheet and found it lacking: I had ruined my childhood. Worse, I had ruined my life. I thought of myself as a child lost in a haunted maze. At school I had remained aloof. Some of the parents felt sorry for me: "Poor child, growing up without a mother . . ." Others suspected me of being deliberately obtuse. While their children played football or baseball or were busy trading candy and presents, I concealed my shame as best I could: I feigned indifference. I turned my back on them, I daydreamed, I leafed through books. I pretended to be more mature, more conscientious, more serious than my older schoolmates. "That one," they would say, pointing to me, "he is strange." And so I was. Strange because different. I knew that I was punished, cursed. And the more I isolated myself, the more I sank into a precocious grief.

There was no one to talk to. I became silent and gloomy, and seemed to bear a grudge against the entire world. Did I really? I judged myself, I condemned myself; I grew old fast. I knew hardly anything of the surprises, the mischief, the exploits, the complicities and adventures that enrich childhood. And yet, there was no lack of opportunities in Brooklyn: libraries and museums, swimming pools and amusement parks, ball games, bowling alleys and the warships, the tall sailing vessels or simply the drugstore next door. Coca-Cola and potato chips, Hershey bars and chewing gum. The street offered a thousand adventures for schoolboys. You meet somebody, you buy a pocketknife, you trade a balloon, you fight, you make up. There were constant battles between clans and tribes with elusive victories and defeats on all sides: I was never involved.

"Oh, yes," says my father, "nothing is as good as silence. But . . ."

He pauses before he continues:

"It is possible to overdo it, do you know that? Silence is a fragile thing."

No, I did not know that. I did not know anything: that was the end result of the most important period of my life. Could it be that I had learned nothing, had absorbed nothing in school?

And where did faith come into all this, my faith in God?

Attending, as I did, an Orthodox day school—ines-
capable in Brooklyn—I began to ask myself the questions that preoccupy children: Good and Evil, the finite
and infinity, the purpose of life and of creation, the
mystery of the suffering of Just Men. I had glanced at
Maimonides' *Guide for the Perplexed* without understanding it. "You are too young for philosophy," my tutor
had said. Poor fellow, he lacked perspective. "Wait till
you're forty," he tried to tell me. "For the answers?"
"No, for the questions." I started looking for another
tutor. One I turned up was an old bachelor who decided to initiate me into astrology. Another wanted to
dispatch me to Nepal. Simha, my father's friend, always managed to bring me back to the straight and
narrow. One day, I confided my doubts to him: why
would the Creator pay attention to this wretched
human dust that worships and defies Him? God is God
and the world is impoverished: the dividing line cuts
through every being, every consciousness. "Simha, tell
me, what is the meaning of all this?" Simha listened to
me at length, patiently, his face shining with pride: "I
like your questions," he said. "What about the answers,
Simha?" "They exist, and they have nothing to do with
your questions."

And so, that particular Friday night I decided I
should perhaps open myself to my father. Confide in
him my panic in the face of the immutable and vexing
laws of creation. Ask for his help. After all, the next day
was going to be special. I deserved some consideration.
But my father was even more somber than usual. I
chose to wait, to remain silent.
At the table, we sang the customary melodies in
honor of *Shabbat* but our hearts were not in it. Our

thoughts were drifting far away and we were anxious to follow them. From time to time I shook myself and stared at the candles whose flames flickered and danced and danced.

"You're thinking of your mother."

"Yes," I admitted, surprised.

My mother, my poor sick mother only rarely came up in our conversations. She was present but as in filigree, as through a screen.

"That's good," said my father. "Tonight you do well to think of your mother."

"Not only tonight," I said. "I often think of her. Almost all the time."

"That's good," said my father reflectively. "That's very good."

"I also think of something else."

His mind elsewhere, he did not hear me the first time. I had to repeat:

"I said that I also think of something else."

"I see," he said. "What exactly are you thinking of?"

"Oh, lots of things."

"Me too."

Were we thinking of the same things? One more question added to all those tormenting me that Friday night before my *Bar Mitzva*. Once again I realized how little I knew of my father, of his past. How many times had I asked him to tell me about my grandparents? About his own activities before the war? "You're too young." I was always too young. Well, now I no longer was: at thirteen it was my duty, therefore my right, to know.

"Father . . ." I began.

He had not heard me. He was off in a distant universe. And where did I fit in? I wanted to be part of it.

"Father," I repeated. "Speak to me."

"You are . . ."

"Don't tell me that I'm too young. Tomorrow I shall assume my responsibilities as a Jew before Israel and the God of Israel. I deserve your confidence, Father. Speak to me."

The candles continued their dance and so did the shadows and my thoughts: they all seemed reflected on my father's pale ascetic face. Suddenly, his breathing became labored: I feared a heart attack. Already I regretted having had the audacity to provoke him, but how could I undo what I had done?

"Sometimes I feel remorse," said my father almost inaudibly.

"Remorse?" I exclaimed. "For what?"

"For many things," he said.

We were still seated at the table, we had not yet said grace. The candles were glimmering, the shadows were slowing down, a song of *Shabbat* wafted in from a nearby apartment. And inside me anxiety was growing, overflowing. My mother's place was here, she deserved to take part in the event, to share this *Shabbat* with her husband and her son. And my father, what was he thinking about?

"Yes," he repeated, "for many things."

"What things?" I asked point-blank.

An iron fist was pounding inside my chest. My father was finally going to lift the veil, I felt it. And I no longer knew whether that was what I wanted. I could still stop the mechanism that would transport me to that awesome, timeless place. All I had to do was to begin clearing the table, to start singing the *Birkat Hamazon,* or to evoke the next day's ceremony. But I wanted to know.

"You are . . . you are too young to know," my father said once again.

He had been so very close. He had changed his mind at the last moment. When would the next opportunity arise?

"You spoke of remorse," I said.

"So I did."

His breath had quickened again. He was closing and opening his eyes as if the light was hurting them. Then he resigned himself to keeping his lids half-closed. And softly, gravely, in short, staccato sentences, he began to recount to me his first years in the United States.

They had been difficult years of adaptation and integration: he had to forget everything, erase everything to start again from zero. Without money or connections, he earned a meager living as a traveling salesman, insurance agent, employee of a cosmetics company. He was hired everywhere but also fired everywhere because of a pathological shyness which arose from the fact that he expressed himself poorly in his new language, perhaps because he respected it too much. Every sentence he spoke had to be correct, well-constructed, flawless. People lost patience and threw him out. He would return a day later or a week later: "You again?!" He would apologize, say thank you and slink away in shame. In the evening, my mother would denounce his failures: "Why can't you be like everybody else? Everybody accepts financial aid from this Jewish agency or that charitable organization, but you have to refuse!" "I don't want to beg." "Is this the time to act proud?" "That's not the point." "Then what is the point?" "It may have been a mistake for us to come to America.

Here, we have nobody." "And there?" "There neither, but it's not the same." My mother agreed on that point: it was not the same.

"There are times," he continued, "when I question whether I did right to rebuild a home, whether I had thought it through when I decided to start our lives over again. Of course, being a Jew bound to his tradition and rooted in its history, I had no choice: others have started over before me, perhaps even for me. What right had I to separate myself from them?

"And yet I continue to have doubts: why didn't I draw the line and end it all? It would have been so easy, so comfortable to let myself be carried by the current of death, to glide into nothingness. Yet I held on. Why? To preserve my name? And ensure the continuity of ancient stock? Or did I wish to rehabilitate my despair by conferring upon it a meaning? Words, words: and they're not even mine. If I am to believe our Sages, *we* are responsible for ultimate redemption. Ask Simha, he will explain it to you: every one of us can bring forth if not the Messiah then perhaps the one who can make Him appear. Is that why we decided, your mother and I, to embrace once more? To entrust you with a messianic mission? With your help to perhaps curb human suffering? Words, more words. We embraced because we were unhappy; we embraced and we were still unhappy.

"And you, my son, what are you doing, what can you do to be happy? I fear that one day you will reproach me for my naiveté and call it weakness. A thoughtless act? No. Rather an act of faith on our part, believe me. Your mother and I told ourselves that not to give life was to hand over yet another victory to the enemy. Why permit him to be the only one to multiply and bear fruit? Abel died a bachelor, Cain did not: it falls to us to correct this injustice. But we did not take into consideration your desires, your judgments, your impulses: and what if one day you tell us, you tell *me*; 'You were wrong to take me into this game you seem to be playing with fate and history! Haven't you learned *anything*? Don't you, didn't you know, that this earth and this society are inhospitable toward Jewish children? Didn't you know that the game was rigged? We had no chance of winning! The enemy is too powerful, and we not enough. One thousand children are helpless against one armed assassin! And so, for you, it was a matter of starting over in the purest sense, wasn't it? Well then, couldn't you start over *without me*?' This is what worries me, my son: that your judgment of our survival may be harsh. And if, God forbid, you give in to despair, my own will be seven times as black. How is one to foresee, how is one to know?"

And as he talked, I listened to him with my head bowed, afraid to meet his gaze. I who so wanted to share the events he concealed, now admitted to myself that they were too much for me. What to do? How could I show him that I loved him even more for it? What could I say to alleviate his pain? I kept silent and listened, I listened long after he had finished speaking.

My father, in fact, behaves and expresses himself freely only with his friend—and mine—Simha. Simha-the-Dark. A soothing, familiar presence. Simha alone knows how to make my father unwind. He brings grace into our home. We are fortunate: he spends all Jewish holidays and many a *Shabbat* with us. He is never intrusive. I look forward eagerly to his visits, and wish only that they were more frequent. He never comes empty-handed. Everything I own—my watch, my fountain pen, my wallet—I received from him.

His presence reassures me I feel closer to him than others do to their "close" relatives. I know many things about him. I know that he is a widower; that he lives in a huge apartment that is off limits to strangers, meaning nearly everybody; that he is a familiar figure in a variety of circles; that he sometimes disappears for weeks at a time without a trace. What else? God only knows what else I know about him. My father thinks of him as a kabbalist. Mathematician and philosopher, a specialist in the theory of possibilities, his free evenings are spent calculating the time that separates us from messianic deliverance.

Where did he get his nickname? He is a nocturnal character attracted by darkness and its ghosts. He calls himself, don't laugh, a merchant, yes, a merchant of shadows. I know it sounds childish, but that is what he claims as his occupation, his profession and, believe it or not, his source of income. He buys and sells shadows, recruiting his clients in every imaginable sphere of American society. It seems that a great industrialist was observed visiting him secretly. As was a movie star. And even a corrupt politician.

One day, he explained his trade to me:

"In America everything is for sale because anything can be bought. Some people cannot live without shadows so they come looking for me. I have what they need. Shadows of every kind. Large and small, opaque and transparent, strong and tired ones, I even have them in colors."

Surely I must have been gaping foolishly because he pretended to be annoyed.

"What, you don't understand? What is there to understand? Business is business. Business is the same everywhere. Some industries sell light, so surely I have the right to sell shadows, don't you think?"

"Of course," I said.

"Why should there be dream merchants, image, illusion, happiness and even death merchants and no shadow merchants?"

I still didn't know whether he was serious.

"Makes sense," I said to show I was not entirely unsophisticated.

"Most people think that shadows follow, precede or surround beings or objects; the truth is that they also surround words, ideas, desires, deeds, impulses and memories. The most exalted faith, the most inspired songs have their share of shadow. God alone has none. Do you know why? God has no shadow because God *is* shadow, hence His immortality. For there exists an ancient belief that man is inseparably and irrevocably linked to his shadow; whosoever separates himself from it would do well to prepare for the great voyage."

Simha and his darkness; Simha and his problems. Once one of his clients wanted to sue him, claiming that Simha had sold him defective merchandise. The second-rate, sickly shadow had vanished after only a week.

"I offered to exchange it. Nothing doing! The client had become attached to his shadow; so help me, he loved it. How can one love a shadow that has disappeared, a dead shadow? People are strange. My client had the audacity to send over a police inspector. Listen, I told him in Yiddish, if you don't clear out this minute, I'll open my warehouse, and unleash my shadows, and

they will overrun the town, the country, the continent
and that will be the end, the end of the world!"

The two friends are in the habit of meeting regularly
on the last Thursday of every month, in our house, in
the living room, to study ancient history or current
events from which they always glean accounts of capital punishment: the process is always the same, so is the
speech. They search heaven and earth to justify a particular act of vengeance against an acknowledged
enemy. Watching them as they sit around the big table
covered with documents and press clippings, listening
to their discussions, one might suspect them of being
involved in a conspiracy or plotting a putsch. Isolated
from the noises of the neighborhood, they seem to exist
in a world all their own, in a time all their own.

"Let us consider the case of our Master, the Master of
all of us, Moses," says Simha. "Let us reread the text,
shall we? Moses is a prince but through his origins and
his soul he is linked to his oppressed brethren. One day
he notices an Egyptian overseer striking his Jewish
slave. In a fit of rage, Moses kills the Egyptian. The
question I am asking you, Reuven Tamiroff, is one you
can guess: what right had Moses to execute the overseer? True, the man had struck a Jew, but did that
crime deserve capital punishment? Tell me?"

As for me, I sit there quietly beneath a worn medieval map of Jerusalem and listen to the prosecution and
the defense, the reading of the same Biblical or Talmudic sentence at the first or third degree, and I am spell-
bound: they are dealing with the incident as if it had
just taken place right here on Bedford Avenue, and
what is more, as if they had just discovered it.

"Whatever Moses did, he was compelled to do," affirms my father. "You see in him only the prophet impassioned with legislation, poetry, teaching, but in fact, he was also a warrior, strategist and military leader. A hero of the resistance. A commander of a national liberation army. He sees an enemy soldier interrogating a Jew; he eliminates him and he is right. Why did the Egyptian abuse the Jew? Possibly to extract secrets from him. Or else to humiliate him and make him into an example to frighten other slaves. Just let them raise their heads and they would suffer the same fate. A killer, once started, will go on killing. A torturer free to torture me today, will turn on you tomorrow. In other words, Moses had to kill the killer to protect not only the present victim but also all future victims."

Logic, one of my father's strengths. He dissects thoughts like a surgeon opening an abdomen to extirpate a disease he alone can see. A method Simha opposes vigorously: every living thought necessarily contains its share of disease, that is to say: its antithought. Better not to tamper with it.

"What troubles me in this particular instance," says my father, "is our vanity: we compare ourselves to Moses. No more, no less. However, what is permissible for Moses is permissible only for Moses. If Moses decides to eliminate a swine, and a dangerous one to boot, that's his right, which does not mean that we are granted the same right."

"Why not? Moses' Law is our Law! It belongs to all of us! Since Sinai . . ."

"Indeed. Since Sinai, the Law does not distinguish between Moses and any simple, anonymous man. But the incident we are considering took place before Sinai! In pharaonic Egypt, killing was not a crime. A prince could kill with impunity; no one could guess that this would change."

"But then, how is it that God, in order to make His Law known, had recourse to a man with blood on his hands?"

"Wait a minute! God forgave Moses and you don't? Do you consider yourself more just than God?"

"Right you are. Moses' 'murder' does not count, does not affect the scheme of events. It is not part of any great pattern because it was Moses who committed it. Had it been you and I, God surely would have put us through the mill."

"Careful there! The Talmud claims that Moses could not enter the Promised Land precisely *because* he had shed blood. Even Moses had no right to kill. In other words, God did not forgive, not completely. And yet, at the moment it took place, the murder seemed necessary if not indispensable, thus justified."

"Justified perhaps, *just* never."

"Because?"

"Because, and this is the essential point, we have not yet established premeditation on Moses' part."

"Premeditation? Impossible! One instant before the murder, Moses could not foresee it. He didn't even know that he would see an Egyptian torturing his Jewish slave."

That's how it went. This is a sample of their sessions which, very seriously, they labeled "official." They continued into the night and sometimes until daybreak. And now, as I recall them, I have the feeling of living in a faraway region shrouded by a dream that disfigures the living and their words. And I hurry away in search of another place, another time, another dream.

WITH THE EXCEPTION of his friend from Davarowsk, my father sees few people. In New York that is easy; you can live in a building for ten years and not know your next-door neighbor. The city is made to order for misanthropes.

For entertainment, we look out the window. Friday nights we go next door to attend services. I do find the Rabbi appealing: I like his beard, his bushy eyebrows. His entire being radiates kindness. His gentleness is legendary, as is his inflexibility. His kingdom is limited but filled with light.

How can I explain the attraction he holds for my father? He reminds him of the old days, the Old World. On Friday nights, carried by his prayers, my father reenters his childhood. As for me, I do not pray; I watch and I listen.

I alternately look at my father and the Rabbi, and I look for a sign from one or the other, a sign meant for me, for me alone.

I like to observe the Rabbi. Mostly he holds himself still and straight as a pillar. When he sways back and forth, he resembles a father trying to soothe his anxious child.

Even though he is demanding, he is loved and respected by his faithful. For he does not push them to saintliness or perfection, only to fervor. One evening he said:

"Whatever I wish to obtain from you, I wish to obtain with you. I wish to see you united so that we may lift ourselves up toward God."

He bowed his head. After a moment he continued:

"You will ask me: how is it possible and what good is it to lift ourselves up to God who is everywhere and not only high above? Well, I don't know the answer but I shall continue to encourage you to look for it."

I remember: I was as moved by his humility as by his determination. I also remember that this was a thought he had put forth more than once. And I who do not like repetition was never troubled by his.

After my father, it was he I loved the most. For his piety? And his wisdom? Undoubtedly. But also for his sense of humor. One holiday eve I heard him speak of misery and suffering:

"The Almighty, blessed-be-He, is a kind of banker. He takes from one man to lend to another, except when it comes to worry, pain, disease: of those He has enough for everybody."

Another time, he commented on the Biblical verse: "And you shall love your fellow man as you love yourself for I am your Lord, your God."

"At first glance," he said, "the sentence is badly constructed: where is the connection between beginning and end? Well, this question has already been posed by the great Rabbi of Rizhin himself. And by way of answer, he told a story: in czarist Russia, there lived two Jews who had vowed to remain friends unto death. And

so, when one of them was accused of subversive activities, the other hastened to exonerate him by taking the
charges upon himself. Of course they wound up in
prison together. The judges were obviously confused:
how could they condemn two men for the same crime?
The case attracted the Czar's attention. He ordered the
two Jews brought before him and this is what he said to
them: 'Don't worry, I am going to set you free. The reason I asked to see you is that I wished to meet two men
capable of such great loyalty. And now,' continued the
czar, 'I have a favor to ask of you: take me as your third
partner.' Commented the Rabbi of Rizhin: This is the
deep and beautiful meaning of that Biblical verse:
when two people love one another, God becomes their
partner."

I remember: I was a youngster when I heard our
neighbor tell this story. And I told myself: when I grow
up I shall love him as I shall love myself. And even
more, if possible.

"Father, may I ask you a question?"
"Of course."
"My schoolmates, for the most part, have grandpar-
ents; I don't. Where are they?"
"Dead," says my father.
"Why?"
"Because they were Jews."
"I don't see the connection."
"Neither do I," says my father.
Oh well, one more question that will go unanswered.
My father is working; I won't disturb him any further. I
go away, come back.

"Do you have any photographs?"

"Of whom?"

"Of my dead Jewish grandparents."

"No," says my father.

All right, I shall go. No, not yet:

"Would you do me a favor?"

"I can try."

"Tell me what they were like."

My father turns thoughtful.

"Different," he says. "Totally different from each other."

"But you just said that they were Jews so they were not different. If they had been, they would not have died. Do you want me to believe that dead Jews are different one from the other?"

"Their life-styles were different. My parents were outgoing and exuberant; your mother's parents preferred understatement. My parents spoke Yiddish, your mother's spoke Polish and German. My parents recited psalms all day long, your mother's did not even know the *Aleph-Beth*. My parents strove to become better Jews, your mother's didn't like Jews; I mean to say: they didn't like the Jew inside them. In truth, they were not pleased with their daughter's choice. They would have preferred a totally assimilated lawyer or even a Gentile of good stock. You must not hold that against them, they were not the only ones. Those were times when people like them said: the world does not tolerate Jews and ultimately will eliminate them. Conclusion: to live, to go on, it was necessary to give up that which had helped us survive two thousand years of exile. Don't you understand? I told you: I myself was briefly tempted, seduced by assimilation. But all I had to do was to remember my father's face—to imagine his despair—in order not to commit the irreparable."

All right, I'll leave you now. To summarize: I had grandparents who wanted to be Jews and grandparents who did not. But they were all killed. Because they were Jews. One last question:

"Since we are Jews, how come we are not dead?"

"Because something in us is stronger than the enemy and tries to be stronger than Death itself."

"I hope so."

But I was far from sure.

My paternal grandparents, simple, honest farmers, lived in Kamenetz-Bokrotay, a village near Davarowsk. They were proud of their son and yet his success frightened them: would it not turn his head and empty his heart? Already his visits were becoming fewer; could he be ashamed of their poverty? The problem was time, he said, there was not enough of it. The curse of success, the price of triumph: no chance to enjoy it. In truth, he seemed depressed, troubled by unspoken worries. What good was praying for him to win his battles if they made him unhappy? They went on praying anyway, my grandparents; they prayed for the continued ascent of their son's star, and never mind the envious.

My father had come to announce his decision to get married, but he had not brought his fiancée. "Her name is Rachel." First lie; her name was Regina. "Are you sure she is for you? That she was meant for you? We so would have liked to choose a wife worthy of you." In their world it was indeed a choice traditionally made by the parents. That was only the first blow. Others followed: my father did not consult them either about the date or the place of the wedding. And he did nothing to bring the future in-laws together. "But who are they?" "Important people." "Are they good people?" "Yes." "Observant Jews?" "They are Jews." Never mind, thought my paternal grandparents, as long as their son was happy. . . . "Are you happy, Reuven?" He was, or at least he said he was. If only he could serve as bridge between two worlds, between two families so far removed one from the other. He imagined an impossible, improbable conversation between his father and his mother-in-law. No, better not to think about it. "We shall overcome the obstacles, won't we, Regina?" "What obstacles?" "I told my parents that your name is Rachel." "Why did you lie?" "I didn't want to hurt them." "What fault could they find with Regina?"

They had met at the university. Both knew discrimination as members of a minority; they spoke, they went out, they loved. Regina's parents opposed the marriage: they would have preferred a wealthier boy but, most of all, one who was less Jewish, meaning one whose family was less embarrassing. Regina was stubborn and pleaded her cause. Reuven was brilliant and he did the rest.

On the appointed day, shortly before the ceremony, my grandfather took his son aside:

"May I speak to you a few minutes?"

"Today? Now?"

"Now."

"Is it so urgent?"

"It may be my only, my last chance."

My father shrugged in resignation as if to say: all right, if you must.

"Listen, my son. You are entering a world which is not mine, one that makes me feel like an intruder. I say to myself: it doesn't matter, he will be happy, he will be happy without me. But I do have a request, my son: don't seek your happiness too far away from us; your mother and I could not bear it. Look: where are your aunts, your uncles, your cousins? Look at us: we are having a celebration—and our closest kin are absent! That signifies something, son, tell me what? I am not educated enough to understand it all: explain it to me."

As he talked, my grandfather had touched his son's shoulder, then his hand rose to his face to stroke it one last time.

"Explain. . . . You cannot? You'll tell me: there are things that cannot be explained? Like love? And happiness? Maybe. You probably know better than I. Still, there is something else: not a question just a prayer: try to remain Jewish. I'm not asking you to grow a beard or to obey the *613* commandments of the Holy Law; I only ask you to remain within that Law. Remember that, Reuven. Remember that, remember us most of all when you're far away from us."

My father never forgot.

As a child and even as an adolescent, I accompanied my father to his place of work in Manhattan: a neighborhood public library, part of the municipal network whose main branch is not far from Times Square. There I would leaf through various illustrated volumes of geography or science fiction, moving from century to century and from personality to personality. I loved those books. To show my gratitude I helped my father by dusting them.

One day I witnessed an extraordinary scene: a burly,

purposeful-looking man walked up to my father and shouted:

"Reuven!"

"Shshsh!"

"Reuven! For God's sake, this is not a cemetery! I've just found you again, I'm happy and you say shshsh?"

"If you don't lower your voice, they'll fire me."

"Don't worry, you'll work for me."

My father closed the file he was studying and motioned me over.

"I'm going out for a few minutes; wait for me."

"Is that your son?"

"Yes."

"I didn't know."

"How could you?"

I couldn't understand why this casual exchange troubled me. I looked the visitor over. Everything about him was oversized: the shoulders, the chin, the mouth and even his gestures.

"I don't want to stay alone," I said.

"But you won't be alone."

"Yes. Without you, I'm alone."

"Let him come along," said the visitor.

He gave me his hand; it felt powerful and warm.

"My name is Bontchek. Your father and I are old friends. We haven't seen each other in years and years, isn't that so?"

"Yes."

They exuded such a feeling of intimacy that it made me feel superfluous; I followed them, staying a few steps behind. And yet how I would have loved to hear what they were saying. Here and there I overheard a few words: "Do you remember the meeting when . . ." "And the day that idiot of a . . ." How could I ever piece it all together? Bontchek did it for me. I saw him often. He came to visit us. He knew Simha-the-Dark. But for reasons I didn't understand yet, he did not attend the monthly reunions. He always appeared unannounced, taking me to the Yiddish Theater in which he invested heavily, or to concerts of liturgical music. He gave me candy and books and spoke to me of many things: of prewar Davarowsk, the vanished Jewish province, of summer gardens and winter mountains. With his descriptions he brought to life for me an entire society with its heroes and villains, its giants and its dwarfs. It was he who described to me, in detail, my parents' wedding.

And what followed.

The war: the separation. That's what war is above all else: separation. Couples that come apart, vows that are undone. You shall love me till death do us part? Of course, I shall love you till death do us part. You'll be careful? Of course, I'll be careful. The train leaves the station and all at once you are swept up in a new rhythm. Nothing is as before: you must please the corporal, learn the art of orienting yourself in the dark, it is all a question of survival.

Reuven Tamiroff is drafted and leaves to join the army. There he volunteers for the front lines, determined to be a hero. Rarely tired, never at rest. At first, his fellow officers make fun of him: "Really, this son of rabbis is trying to give us lessons in patriotism!" Then their mockery turns into grudging acceptance: "Never mind his motives, fact is: he's not a coward, not like the rest of them." In the end, one or two of them offer him their friendship.

The Polish army is waging a valiant battle, sacrificing the elite of its troops and cavalry, but it is behind by a war or two: the invader crushes it with its weight of steel. Cities and fortresses are falling one after the other; everywhere there is retreat; everywhere there is defeat, sorrow, sadness, humiliation.

One month of captivity. Anxiety. Escape. Reuven Tamiroff, two military medals in his backpack, returns to Davarowsk, races home, finds the apartment empty. Regina, where is Regina? He races on toward the villa: his in-laws seem unprepared for his miraculous return; they congratulate him on his bravery on the battlefield but do not invite him to sit down. As a matter of fact, he would do better to head straight for Bokrotay, to his parents: that is where Regina is.

Head for Bokrotay? Not easy. The occupying forces have confiscated every automobile and every horse. Finally, Reuven does find a bicycle: one hour later, exhausted, he pushes open the door of the house where he was born. His mother is crying, his father is reciting a prayer. Regina, stunned at first, grabs him by the arm and drags him outside, into the garden: there they embrace with a passion that surprises them both.

"Why didn't you stay at home?"

"I was afraid."

"Of whom? For whom?"

"I was afraid."

"You should have moved in with your parents."

"I chose to come and live with yours."

Regina explains. She is ashamed to explain but she cannot avoid it:

"It's not nice, but I can't help it; before the Germans arrived I suggested to my parents to invite yours, to offer them shelter. God knows the villa is large enough for all of us to be comfortable in it. My father looked at me as if I'd gone mad, as if I'd demanded he distribute his wealth to the poor, or decided to invite the butcher to lunch. 'You're losing your mind,' he answered with his usual arrogance: 'Can you see us associate with those people?' 'But they're my family! They're in danger!' 'You need rest,' said my father. 'Go and lie down; tomorrow you'll feel better.' And so I got angry. I left the villa slamming the doors. And here we are. A little walk never hurt anybody."

My father is flustered, unable to express his feelings in words. He loves his wife more than ever; he loves her with a love that is physical but much more: thinking of her is as exciting as touching her.

"Be proud of your Rachel," my grandfather tells him. "We are."

And after a pause:

"In our tradition it is the woman who represents continuity; it is she who carries and projects the future of our people. And that is how it should be. Don't you agree?"

"Yes. I agree."

A memory: wrapped in a heavy shawl, my father is working, I look at him, I observe him as he scribbles notations in the margins of his favorite book and I am moved. Suddenly, inexplicably, I feel like teasing him:

"You rediscovered him, you retranslated him, fine. But you no longer teach ancient literature! You're no longer in Davarowsk! Admit that it's funny: you live in Brooklyn, the Hasidic center of the universe, and you continue to regard Paritus as a guide, a Master!"

My remarks were not malicious. But my father looks troubled.

"All ideas reflect the same Idea, the same Idea of the Idea; every life testifies to the same Creator. You are free to synthesize them; more than that: you are free to live that synthesis. 'Every point is a point of departure,' said Paritus."

"Why choose between two roads if they lead to the same destination?"

"You misunderstand my thought. I don't like to leave, I don't like to return. Yet I am returning."

And, shyly, he adds:

"Just as your mother did."

YOUR FATHER has changed," Bontchek was telling me. "All of us have changed. First of all, we were younger. But there is something else: we lived a great and awesome adventure. Eternal salvation and damnation lived side by side in every one of us and particularly in your father. He was our leader, you didn't know that, did you? Admit it: you didn't know. And yet, son, it's the truth. Your father, an expert in ancient texts, woke up one morning with a mandate from history to lead his people and spare it a death that modern science had perfected to a degree never before attained.

"I remember the first time I saw him in that role: we had been summoned by the military governor of Davarowsk, Richard Lander, whom we called the *Angel*, who wished to communicate to us his plans regarding the future—or lack of future—of the community. We were there, some twelve men, facing a high SS officer and we wondered whether we would see our families again. We knew that in a neighboring village *they* had recently assembled twenty-four Jewish notables for a so-called 'work session'; their corpses had been returned to the community the following day against payment of one hundred thousand marks. On what basis had we been chosen? Nobody knew. I myself represented a youth movement. But there was also the director of the Jewish hospital. And the president of the community. And the representative of the American *Joint Distribution Committee*. And Rabbi Aharon-Asher. And, of course, your father. Did I say: of course? I meant to say the opposite. He was not active in the community, I don't even know whether he was a member, I mean: a registered member. But he was known. A personality. Notwithstanding his age he had already achieved celebrity thanks to his work on an obscure Latin philosopher whose name escapes me now.

"Well, the officer delivered a speech that made us shiver: on behalf of the German occupation authorities, he was transmitting orders we were to carry out without discussion: any failure to do so would be punishable by our collective death. For, from that moment on, we had become a Jewish Council, a sort of autonomous governing body for the Jewish inhabitants of Davarowsk. One of us dared submit his resignation: it was, I think, the Joint Committee emissary. The governor, polite but cold, asked to be told his reason. 'Because, sir, it is required by my official position. I do, after all, represent a foreign organization.' 'I see,' said the officer calmly, 'I see.'

"He did not pick up his revolver, he contented himself with glancing at it as though soliciting its advice: 'Here,' he said so quietly that we had to make an effort to hear him, 'nobody resigns without my authorization. You do nothing without my authorization. In this place I decide whether you live or die. It is my prerogative to evaluate your logic, your reasoning, your hopes, your behavior, your desires, your jealousies, your anxieties, it is I and only I who will determine their intensity and

their duration. Have I made myself sufficiently clear?'
The Joint emissary, relying on his affiliation with powerful America, was about to answer. I yanked his sleeve
and may have saved his life. 'Very well,' said the governor. 'Now we need a president.' And since nobody
moved, he continued: 'No council can function without
a president. So, who wishes to volunteer?' Naturally,
nobody raised a hand: we would have each preferred to
die. We knew instinctively: a president who presides at
the pleasure of the enemy, eventually tries to please the
enemy. And none of us wished to sink that low.

" 'In that case,' said the governor, 'I shall make the
decision: you,' he said, pointing his finger in the di-
rection of Rabbi Aharon-Asher. 'You are a rabbi, you
will know how to make yourself respected.' A heavy silence fell on us. The SS officer was looking at the Rabbi
but we were looking at the black revolver on the table,
within his reach. The Rabbi would refuse, that was
predictable. And his refusal would cost him, would cost
us, dearly, our lives perhaps. If only I were not able to
foresee the future, I thought angrily. If only I could
muzzle my imagination. In my mind's eye I visualized
the scene about to unfold: the Rabbi would say 'No,'
and the officer without losing his terrifying calm, would
kill him on the spot, like that, standing up. Indeed, the
Rabbi said 'No,' that is to say, he shook his head which
was beautiful, radiating kindness and strength. 'How
dare you?' said the officer. 'I named you president and
you have the audacity to decline this honor? Do you realize that through my person and my position you have
just insulted the army of the Third Reich and its beloved Führer?'

"He still had not raised his voice. For me, that was a
sign that he surely was a professional who would kill in
cold blood, with efficiency and precision, without hate,

I would even say: without passion. Didn't the Rabbi understand that? Why didn't he accept the order, even if it meant shedding the stupid presidency later? 'I'd like to explain my refusal,' he said, 'but I do not speak German.' The director of the Jewish hospital volunteered to translate from the Yiddish; the officer gave his silent consent. 'The honorable governor says that I would know how to make myself respected. That is correct. But I have absolutely no need of another title to be respected. The one I bear will do. I promise you to put it to good use. Having said that, I would like, with your permission, sir, to draw your attention to the following fact: in my capacity as Rabbi, I have authority over the religious Jews but not over the others. Therefore you need—forgive me; *we* need—somebody no segment of the community can object to.' Strange, but the officer swallowed the argument. And that is how your father, the famous interpreter of the Latin philosopher with the name nobody could ever remember, was designated chief of his community.

"As he left the Town Hall transformed into Kommandantur, your father challenged the Rabbi rather rudely, but I understood him: 'What you have done is not right, Rabbi,' he said; 'you extricated yourself knowing that in so doing, you were naming somebody else to your post. You did not have the courage to fulfill your duties, Rabbi, and that troubles me. I took you for an honest man, a man of integrity. I was wrong about you; you are seeking nothing but ease and comfort. You like others to do the dirty work for you so that you may devote yourself to God. I only hope that God will reject you, that He will not want a hypocrite of your kind!' Oh, yes, he really let him have it, your father; we all stood there aghast. Pale but composed, the Rabbi did not turn his back on him nor did he interrupt; on the contrary, he listened till the end with a growing and painful intensity. Then he answered him: 'I understand your disappointment, my young friend. You judge me and you are severe. Would you permit me to explain? I promise to be brief. To spare the community I would gladly have accepted the post. Believe me, I refused only because my being a rabbi would limit me in the exercise of those functions: I would be obliged to consult the books of *Halakha* from morning till night, for every small detail and, I know it already, we are about to live through singular times; we shall have to confront situations never conceived of in our books. Any one among us is better equipped than I am to fulfill the task, because he is not a rabbi, as you are not. But I shall help you, I promise solemnly: I shall remain at your side. To the end.' He paused a moment as if to measure the words he had just pronounced.

" 'To the end,' he repeated."

"Do you remember, Reuven?" Bontchek asked again. "We were going from miracle to miracle. You crossed the street without getting shot? A miracle. You met an SS officer and you were still able to go home? An even greater miracle. God was hiding behind His miracles. The *Angel* demanded two hundred and fifty furs? We had only half that. And yet, at the appointed time, they were all delivered. And the boxes of silver. And the dollars, the napoleons. How did you accomplish so many miracles, Reuven, you who, at least at that time, did not believe in them?"

"Be quiet," said my father, suddenly grim.

"But your associate, Rabbi Aharon-Asher, the

grandson of the famous preacher of the same name, *he* believed."

"Be quiet," repeated my father. "The Rabbi was a saintly man. You have no right to ridicule a saintly man who is no longer of this world."

"Was it he who brought you back to faith? If so, then I am right in saying that he performed miracles!"

It was Friday night. We were four around the table. Simha and my father seemed unusually calm. Simha, who had a good voice, refused to sing the customary hymns. My father barely touched his food. Only Bontchek, who was slightly drunk, appeared to be in a good mood:

"Do you remember the *Angel?* Tell me, Reuven, do you remember him? Handsome man, wasn't he?" Bontchek continued, moving restlessly in his chair. "Always elegant, well-groomed, closely shaven, an intelligent smile, gloved hands. ... A man of culture, and what an education! Unfair, don't you think? Killers should be frightening; our *Angel* inspired confidence."

"Be quiet, Bontchek," said my father. "This is not a proper conversation for *Shabbat.*"

"But it is for a Thursday night, yes? In that case, why don't you invite me for next Thursday?"

My father and Simha exchanged embarrassed glances and said nothing.

"As for me, I find the subject perfectly suitable for the *Shabbat* mood," said Bontchek. "After all, we are talking about an *Angel* and what would *Shabbat* be without the *Shabbat* angels? You see, Reuven, I know a few things. I am not a rabbi but I am smart."

"Shall we go visit the Hasidim?" suggested my father to change the subject.

"Good idea," said Simha. "It seems that the Rabbi of

Belz is here on a visit from Jerusalem. I'd love to see
him hold court."

"His faithful pray very rapidly, they say. The reason:
to outwit the demon who attacks Jewish prayers to prevent them from reaching the celestial throne. The aim
is to finish before he arrives."

"You've already reached heaven?" exclaimed Bontchek. "I'm still in the ghetto."

"Let's go," said Simha. "Let's go to Belz. On the way
we can stop at Lubavitch or Wizhnitz. I love their
songs."

"I'm staying," said Bontchek.

"So am I," I said.

"Don't you want to come with us?" asked my father.
"You usually like to take a walk on Friday nights."

That is true: I usually did. Friday nights in Brooklyn
you walk through a peaceful and melodious universe:
almost like Central Europe before the catastrophe.

"Not tonight," I repeated.

And I remained alone with Bontchek who opened for
me the gates of Davarowsk, where the *Angel* was sover-
eign.

"Would you like me to tell you the story from the beginning? One day, the commandant Richard Lander
appeared in the middle of a session of the Jewish Council to break the news: 'Berlin has ordered me to institute
new regulations which I consider useful. Do you trust
me?' What a question. Of course, the Jewish councillors, the Jewish inhabitants of Davarowsk trusted him:
was he not our protector, our benevolent *Angel*? 'I am

sorry I must point this out to you so brutally, but frankly, the local population is not very fond of you. You cannot imagine the extent, the intensity of its hatred. If we were not here to restrain the mob, you would be in trouble, believe me.'

"We believed him, of course. We sincerely believed him. Protected by the occupier, our former neighbors had removed their masks and covered us with spittle and abuse. After this first statement, the *Angel* launched into a scholarly exposé on the causes of anti-Semitism: 'The hatred that all nations feel for you is, in fact, regrettable but at the same time undeniable. What should one attribute it to? How should one interpret it?' The list was long: greed and hunger for power, abnormal sexual appetites, taste for the occult, for falsehood, for ritual murder; all were invoked. Then came religious quotations, modern slogans; he was in top form, the *Angel*. And as he spoke—and he went on and on, for perhaps two hours—I felt myself overcome with anxiety as at the approach of an implacable threat.

" 'And so,' concluded the *Angel*, 'it was decided in high places to establish, for your protection, a special zone where your enemies shall not be able to pursue you. It bears an ancient name: ghetto.' At last, a smile flickered over his face: he had become aware of the effect of the casually dropped word. I felt a chill. All over. A glacial hand crept down the length of my spine. 'I see that you are pleased,' said the *Angel*. 'That proves to me that I am dealing with men of intelligence and foresight. Bravo! You shall live happy days. Happy and, above all, serene. I promise you: you shall be at home. In your own private little kingdom. You shall see only one person from the hostile outside world: me. Your intercessor. Your faithful friend. Your Guardian *Angel*.' That is how he got his name: *Angel*. The *Angel* of uncer-

tainty. The *Angel* of terror. The *Angel* of death. For we
all knew the true significance of the word ghetto; its
suggestive, destructive power had been etched in our
collective memory for a thousand years. Ghetto meant
solitude, isolation, exile, famine, misery and disease.

" '*When?*' asked your father, his stance more rigid
than ever. '*When* will the ghetto be established? *When*
will the transfer, the population exchange, take place?'
He had asked the questions in a peremptory tone, plac-
ing the emphasis over and over on the *when*; believe me,
it was impressive. 'In one week,' replied the military
governor. 'My staff has laid out the plans. The ghetto
will comprise nine streets.' 'Which ones?' 'The streets
that lead to the Small Market; there are already Jews
living there, that will make things easier.' 'And the
others? Where do you plan to locate all those who live
in other areas?' 'You'll squeeze in somehow, you'll all
be one big family. A little crowded perhaps? So what!
That will be one of the charming aspects of the ghetto:
when people love one another, a little promiscuity
doesn't hurt, quite the opposite.' The *Angel* played his
little comedy straight; not one muscle of his face be-
trayed his irony. Before adjourning the meeting, he
turned to your father and told him: 'And you, in the
kingdom of David, you shall be king.' And to Rabbi
Aharon-Asher: 'And you, you shall be its High Priest.'
Whereupon he burst into laughter. And stupidly, I
swear to you, this laughter reassured me.

"As soon as he left the room, I remarked aloud that
the situation ought not to be viewed too bleakly: the
prospect of Jewish life within a Jewish framework contained certain positive aspects, for . . . One look from
your father made me swallow the rest of my speech.
'What are we going to do?' he asked. The council members were too stunned to respond. Your father was on

the verge of repeating his question when a young
woman came in and whispered in his ear that an important person was waiting for him outside. 'I am busy.'
'I told him that, but he insists.' 'Who is it? A German?'
'No. It's your father-in-law.' Your father went out. Seeing the panic in your maternal grandfather's face—he
was standing there with a handkerchief pressed against
his mouth—your father could not resist striking a blow:
'Well, well, now I've seen everything! You here!' 'True,
I never thought that I would ever set foot in this place!
Really, what a smell! What ugliness! How can you
stand it, my dear son-in-law?' Your father grew impatient: 'You wished to see me urgently, what do you
want?' 'I learned from reliable sources that the occupation authorities plan to establish a ghetto. And force us
to live with . . . with people like these. I have decided to
move to the capital where I can count on support in
high places. Come with us.' And with a sigh: 'And take
your parents too. You see I am less selfish than you
think.'

"Your father felt the blood surge to his face; all kinds
of words were rushing into his head: ghetto and *Kaddish,*
kingdom and cemetery, salvation and escape. Was it
such a simple choice? If your grandfather was right, the
Jewish people was lost: the real Jews would perish; only
renegades like himself would remain. 'I thank you,' he
told him, 'but I cannot.' 'You cannot?' 'I have responsibilities; I am in charge.' 'What about your family?'
'Speak to your daughter. She is free.' 'I have spoken to
her. She refuses to leave you.' Your father smiled a mel-
ancholy smile as if to say: You see? That's how we are.
'You're mad,' said his father-in-law. 'Mad to expose
yourself to unnecessary risks. Mad not to think about
the future, about the generations to come.' 'Mad? Perhaps. But if one day you should meet my teacher and

friend Rabbi Aharon-Asher, ask him to tell you the
story of the fish and the fox.'

"Your grandfather shrugged with disappointment
and disgust, shook his son-in-law's hand and left. Your
father thought he would never see him again; he was
wrong. Two or three months later, the police brought
your maternal grandparents back from the capital.
Like it or not, they were Jews and thus came under the
anti-Jewish laws. Like it or not, their place was inside
the ghetto.

"But I am digressing: let us not forget the *Angel* since
tonight is *Shabbat*. He often came to inspect his kingdom. He appeared to enjoy its squalor, its filth, its pain.
He would let his gaze wander over the alleyways, the
crowded yards, the hovels, the barns that served as
warehouses and shelters. He looked at his creation and
found it satisfactory. He usually chose to come alone
and leave alone. Outside, he hardly ever moved without a host of lieutenants, experts, adjutants and SS orderlies. But inside the walls, he had no one. He came
and went, sometimes stopping to knock at a door, politely asking permission to enter: 'So, there are quite a
lot of you in this one room.' If the residents agreed, they
risked losing one of their own; if instead they protested
that there was room enough, more people were sent in.
The way this was usually handled was to tell him re-
spectfully that he alone was judge of the situation. A
variation on the same theme at the hospital: 'You are
sure, absolutely sure that it would not be better to
transfer some of the gravely ill patients to a better
equipped hospital?'

"But his main performance was reserved for us, the
members of the Jewish Council: a speech on law and
order, a speech on the majesty of power and, for good
measure, the power of majesty; a complaint about the

egoism of the masses who do not sufficiently appreciate the cult of authority, and on the foolishness of the individual who prefers submission to domination. In short, he loved to speak, the *Angel* loved to hear himself speak. As for us, we followed every word, every inflection, with excruciating intensity, knowing that what he said held implications for the survival or extinction of our people. 'For the moment, things aren't going too badly,' commented Rabbi Aharon-Asher after he left. 'He speaks and we listen, he teaches and we learn. That's neither a crime nor a sin. Our immediate duty: vigilance. As soon as we sense a change, we must reconsider. One thing is certain: we shall not become instruments in the hands of the enemy. One other certainty: one day the *Angel* will cease to play and so shall we. That will be the beginning of the true ordeal.' "

"You were wrong not to come with us," says my father returning from Belz. "You would have lived unforgettable moments. This *Shabbat* is unlike any other."

But I see Rabbi Aharon-Asher, I listen to his solemn, reassuring words, I follow him through the crowded alleys of the Davarowsk ghetto whose heartbeat becomes the languid murmur of the sick and I say:

"You are right, Father. This *Shabbat* is unlike any other."

ONCE I feared solitude. I felt evil spirits prowling around me, waiting for me to be alone to pounce on me and take me away. Of course, I never told my father but I managed not to let him out of my sight. I accompanied him everywhere. On the days when I was off from school, I went with him to the library.

"Won't you be bored?"

"No."

"Are you sure?"

"Don't worry about me. I'll read."

In truth, I was happy just to look around.

All those regular visitors to the library, were they aware of the fact that I was observing them? I followed their movements; I observed every one of their gestures, spontaneous or deliberate, as if I had been hired by the police to spy on them. I told myself that the more I learned about them, the more I would know about my father. Of course, for appearance's sake, I accepted the few dollars that the director magnanimously handed to me every month for restoring returned volumes to their proper places; he never would have suspected that my motives were personal and that money was not one of them.

Among the faithful readers there was a woman of a certain age, white-haired, flirtatious; she would sit there, happily reading the same book—a nineteenth-century novel—over and over again. Moved by her constancy, I bought her a copy. A memorable day for her and for me: she refused my gift.

"Young man," said she, "you don't understand these things, you're too young. Do you think I come here to satisfy my literary tastes?"

Indeed, I had been blind: she came because she was in love. Not with that particular novel but with my father.

An elegant man—graying hair, high forehead, silk shirt, fine briefcase—made his appearance every Wednesday at the same hour, 3:14 P.M., opened whatever volume I handed him, had a good cry and left.

Still, the craziest character was a certain Donadio Ganz who claimed to be originally from Safed or Salonika, while at the same time denying, for reasons beyond my understanding, that he was Sephardic. His visits were irregular but memorable. He would wander from section to section, from room to room, haughtily taking in the scenery like a landowner making the rounds of his domain. What he said was unequivocal: "All these books are mine." And so they were, not, mind you, because he had bought and sold them but because . . . because . . . What's wrong with you, don't you understand? It's so simple: these books, he had written them. He? Yes. All of them? All of them. Except for the cookbooks, he would say with a feigned air of modesty. But the historical works, the novels, the medieval poems, Maimonides and Ronsard, Descartes and

Cicero, Cervantes and Bahia ibn-Pekuda: all were his
pseudonyms, that was the truth.

One day I find him sitting by himself at a desk,
immersed in a work by ibn-Gabirol, shaking his head,
visibly distressed; I ask him whether I can be of
help.

"Unfortunately not," says he. "It's my fault. Three
verses have to be rewritten."

Fearing a burst of inspiration on his part, I stay close
by. I worry that he might tear out the few "regrettable"
pages.

"If only I could begin all over again," he sighs. "I
have so much to do, I beg your pardon: redo."

He winks at me. We understand each other. He is
harmless, pathetic, likable, anyway, I love madmen. I
invite him to eat something with me in the cafeteria
next door; it is not easy to sustain an intelligent conversation here in the reading room. . . .

"You are Tamiroff's son," he says. "You deserve the
honor I am doing you by accepting your invitation.
Were I not busy revising myself, I would do a book
about him. What a life he has led!"

"You know it?"

"Do I know it? Who taught him philosophy? And
modern literature? And the occult sciences, who, tell
me, introduced him to them? Why do you think he is
working in *this* library rather than in another? I had, I
have something to do with that."

My luck, I thought. Finally I meet someone who
knows everything about my father and he turns out to
be insane.

Around us, the multilingual voices of the metropolis,
amazing social and ethnic caldron into which new immigrants plunge only to be reborn, able once more to

face life and its obstacles, happiness and its illusions.

I think of my father and also my mother. I know that they played the game, surely my father did, my mother less. I know that they were registered in English courses for adults; that they studied the history, customs and basic laws of this young and hospitable nation. My father was determined and quickly passed his exams; my mother gave up midway. Nevertheless, they reached the same point: together they obtained their green cards, together they became citizens of the United States. I know that for many, many months my father was never without his passport, even when he went to bed.

In the cafeteria I look at the men and women milling about and I feel gratitude toward their country which is also mine.

In one corner, a student from the *yeshiva* across the street is leafing through a seditious pamphlet; from time to time his worried eyes wander over the rest of the room. Any danger? No, no danger. Reassured, he re-opens the small book concealed in the palm of his hand. On the other side of the room, a pair of lovers: the boy is Puerto Rican, the girl looks Scandinavian; they still do not speak the same language but they know what to do; they are embracing; there is no need to say anything, at least not in words.

Donadio Ganz sees nothing. Too absorbed by his own "work," he tells me in detail how the idea came to him to write the *Guide for the Perplexed,* Plato's *Dialogues,* Spinoza's *Ethics;* he describes in detail the damp attic where he dictated portions of his work to the pantheist philosopher. Then he shares with me the true motives of Gérard de Nerval's suicide; nobody knows it, but he, Donadio Ganz, refused to be his ghostwriter. . . .

But, why indeed had he refused him his services? "Ah," says he, "don't you know? Gérard was a night person who didn't believe in sleep whereas I, Donadio, was exhausted and all I wanted was to sleep. . . . By the way, I plan to rework his last poem, I owe him that much. . . ."

THEODOR HERZL says somewhere that nothing that happens is ever as bad as one fears or as good as one hopes. At first that surely was true as far as the Jews of Davarowsk were concerned. The *Angel* had not been entirely wrong: for better or worse, people adjusted to the ghetto, settling into it as into an illness—with the hope of coming out of it sooner or later.

"Be proud of your father," Bontchek tells me; "we all were. First he acted as our buffer, then he helped us not to forget who we were."

He gets excited, Bontchek, when he is singing my father's praises. His warm voice throbs with emotion:

"Thanks to your father we became conscious of our historical obligations. Do you understand that? I, Bontchek, son and grandson of Jewish peddlers from Poland, had never thought of my life, my work or even my Zionist activities in historical terms: I didn't know what that meant: historical considerations. In the movement we discussed politics, pioneering, agriculture and illegal 'excursions' into Palestine. History, as a living crucible for mankind, was made tangible to us by your father. 'One day books will be written about us.' That was his favorite expression. And nobody said: 'What do I care? One hour of joy, of pleasure, one instant of life is worth more than all the dead phrases. . . .'

"On the contrary, we imagined that one day historians would pore over our chronicles, trying to understand, judging perhaps. We expressed our thoughts with greater sincerity, we acted with less carelessness. To accomplish a mission. To benefit by it. Everywhere and in everything, your father served as our role model."

Bontchek, who had become my friend, found in me a faithful and fervent audience. All that my father hides from me out of discretion, he will reveal to me. With him as my guide, I yearn to enter the ghetto and meet its quietly delirious inhabitants. I want to participate in their agony, to be one of them in their struggle. I am determined to hear their morning prayers, to be present at the "shows" produced by their "cultural services," to endure the anguish of the night and the more oppressive torment of dawn. I want to accompany the hungry, the sick, the sad-eyed, wide-eyed madmen, the mute old men, the despairing gravediggers, I want to remember every face, retrieve every tear and every silence, I want to live, to relive my father's experience; without that knowledge, without that fragment of memory acquired after the fact, I can never get close to him, I feel that. There would always be something ineffable between us.

"Thanks to your father," Bontchek continued, "we had learned to experience events in their totality. The daily misfortunes, the individual and collective ordeals, the perils, the threats but also the challenges, the prayers, the acts of solidarity and resistance: you could

never imagine what our days were like. Every time
there was a problem—meaning constantly—or a crisis
erupted—which happened all the time—it was he who
took charge. He was universally trusted. The rich
feared him, the scholars respected him; as for the poor,
they genuinely loved him, worshiped him: he was their
powerful new brother, their loyal and generous brother.
Sure, there were those who were dissatisfied, the chron-
ically disgruntled, that's normal: he could not please
everybody. To be just with one meant being severe with
another. That was the epithet applied to him in the
ghetto: just. He was integrity personified. No little
favors for his friends; no services bought or sold; no discrimination.

"His parents who had been evacuated from their village received the same lodgings in the ghetto as their
neighbors. Like everybody else, his in-laws stood in line
for the various coupons distributed weekly by the Jewish Council. Oh, you should have seen them: assimilated former capitalists, dreadful snobs, thrown in with
refugees in rags, whom just a few weeks before they
would not have deigned to notice. . . . I know, sonny, I
am speaking of your grandparents, I am being disre-
spectful. . . . Forgive me. But they really were ashamed
of their Jewishness, they were Jews who made us feel
ashamed. . . . Not so your father's parents: they were a
beautiful sight to behold, believe me. Never complaining. Never demanding their due. Never trying to influence their son on their own behalf. Funny, as I think of
them I begin to smile."

What about my mother in all this? Why did he never
mention her? I felt that in some obscure way her illness

was profoundly connected with the ghetto and with my
father's refusal to speak of it. I felt that she held the keys
to secrets that were not only her own. How to find out?
How to uncover the first clue? After all, I could not
question a stranger—all right, almost a stranger—
about my parents' past; it would have been indecent.

If, at least, my mother were in good health, if she
lived at home, with us, showered with attention and
care, I might have dared rummage through her life; I
might have found an opportune moment, a plausible
pretext. But her illness demanded a certain respect, a
fundamental reticence. One does not play detective
with a mother under treatment in a clinic. After all,
there are limits . . .

And so I carefully chose detours. I opened many
doors, showed myself interested in a thousand episodes,
asked to learn everything about life in the ghetto. Who
was in charge of food distribution? Of education? Of
shelter?

For example, my voice carefully controlled, I would
ask: "Where did my father live?"

"In a rather modest, not to say shabby apartment.
And you should know that as president of the Jewish
Council he was entitled to an official residence: living
room, bathroom and all the rest. He did not want it. He
preferred a dingy room. There too your peculiar father
with his principles and his taste for justice was set on
showing the way. If the president lived in comfort then
the other council officials, from the highest to the
lowest, would have demanded the same or more. No,
your father opted for simplicity. Austerity. Running
water, yes. Bathroom, no. He came to our house to take
showers. Just like our other colleagues. With one excep-

tion: our Rabbi, who went to the *mikva* every morning for his ritual immersions and ablutions. Otherwise, he said, his prayers would lack purity. You won't believe me, but in winter, in twenty to thirty degrees below zero, this astonishing character went nevertheless to plunge his emaciated body into the icy waters of the *mikva* which, since there was no wood or coal, was impossible to heat. Of course, he was not the only one. There were also some women, few it must be said, who went there to conform to Biblical law."

Since he mentioned women, I seized the opportunity: "You never speak of my mother, did . . ."

"Pious, she? What a strange idea. . . ."

"But . . . what *did* she do in the ghetto? How did she spend her time?"

"She worked. Everybody worked, either for the Germans or for the Jews. Often it was not easy to distinguish between the two employers. The physicians who treated the sick to make them fit for work, were they not helping the Germans, however indirectly, however involuntarily? And yet . . . Could they refuse treatment to the Jews? Those were complicated times indeed. . . ."

"My mother worked at the hospital?"

"At the hospital, too. And in the communal kitchen. And with the staff in charge of shelter. She was treated with great respect as she was neither pretentious nor proud and never took advantage of her privileged situation."

"Did you see her often?"

"Every day."

"Tell me."

"What would you like me to say? She was somebody special."

"More."

"What more do you want?"

"Tell me all you know."

"All days resembled one another in the ghetto. So did the nights. And so did the people. Not so your mother."

"She was different?"

"Yes."

"How?"

"She suffered."

"Surely she wasn't the only one who suffered? How was her suffering different from that of all the other ghetto dwellers?"

Bontchek suddenly turned sullen:

"All suffering is different."

And he changed the subject.

"It's your mother's fault," Lisa said primly. Her manner was both coy and scornful.

"What's my mother's fault?"

"Your shyness."

She looked me over with mock solemnity and with a laugh went on:

"And everything else."

We were attending the same course at City College in New York. She was eighteen. I was much older. Twenty, almost twenty-one. She was the brightest student in class. According to her I was the most reserved, the most inhibited, the most complex-ridden. She was dynamic, frivolous, frenetic, constantly on the lookout for action and adventure, bubbling with curiosity, with yearnings, taking part in every project, every exploit, on condition that it be offbeat. As for me? Just as in school and even in kindergarten before that, I was content to go unnoticed. Neither the professors nor the students knew who I was. More often than not, they were unaware of my very existence, which both troubled and reassured me. But there was Lisa. Lisa who saw everything. Heard everything. And minded everybody's business. Lisa forced me out of anonymity as if she had caught me doing something wrong.

"You are hiding," she exclaimed triumphantly.

"What nonsense," I said blushing.

"You are blushing! You are hiding and blushing! I can't believe my eyes! Where do you come from? Who are you? My name is Lisa, Lisa Schreiber, yes, just like the banker, I am his only child and not a virgin."

All around us, her admirers were shaking with laughter. I didn't know where to run. Awkward and bewildered I stood there stammering incoherently. That only heightened Lisa's amusement. Why was she seeking to humiliate me? To prove she was the stronger? One more minute, one more word and I would have burst into tears. She must have realized it because she ended my agony by taking my hand.

"Come. We are going to spend the evening together."

Disarmed, I let her do as she pleased. As we left, some boys called out to her; she responded alternately with a laugh or a scowl. Outside, the crowded street annoyed her.

"Let's take a taxi. You're broke? I'm not. If you marry me, you'll be making a good deal."

I had never met such a woman. Willful, insolent, brash, not beautiful, the typical sensual redhead, possessive yet endearing with her birdlike movements. Lord, why hast thou forsaken me?

She lived in a town house on Ninetieth Street near Fifth Avenue, a four-story building, half museum, half palace, filled with antique carpets and silver.

"Don't worry," said Lisa. "My parents are not home. My mother is traveling and my father is minding his investments. The perfect couple: he collects millions and she collects lovers. Do I shock you? What's the matter with you, what century do you live in, anyway?"

She pushed me into the kitchen, the bar, the library, opened bottles and jars, talking provocatively all the while, a true whirlwind, and I followed her like a robot or a sleepwalker, wondering what in the world I was doing here, in her home, with her, and also why God had condemned me to aberration and why was my heart pounding so wildly. . . .

"And, in conclusion, the guide will show you the sanctuary: my room. Forgive the mess, but anyhow you and I will make it a little messier yet, all right?"

And without granting me a moment's respite, she challenged me:

"You have a choice. We talk now and make love later or the other way round. You decide."

Earth and heaven collapsed and I felt my knees buckle. My head was swimming and I was gasping for air and all my past years became shrouded and opaque, weighing on me, crushing me.

"I like you," said Lisa as her fingers caressed my hand, my throat, and slowly inched up toward my lips. "I like you because you're shy; you're shy because your mother stuck you with a lot of complexes. We'll make love and you'll tell me about her, all right? No? Then tell me about her, we'll make love later."

Heaven and earth changed places and, becoming one, sank into the same abyss.

Bontchek, though reticent about my mother, seemed fascinated by the strange friendship that had bound

my father to Rabbi Aharon-Asher of Davarowsk.
"They were inseparable. The Rabbi had kept his
word. He was constantly at his protégé's side, advising
him, guiding him, backing him. It was the Rabbi who
encouraged your father to study the Law and its commentaries. 'I am not asking you to practice your religion, only to know it,' he told him. 'Isn't it too late to
start?' asked your father. 'To his last breath, with his
last breath, the Jew can and must pursue knowledge,'
answered the Rabbi. 'The moment before he dies, man
can still discover everything about creation and the
Creator.' And your father obediently began to study
the Bible, the Prophets, the Midrash. Can you imagine
your grandparents' happiness? People once came to tell
them of their son's presence at a *Shabbat* service at the
Rabbi's home. 'I'm going there,' called your grandfather. 'I want to see him, I want to embrace him in front
of everybody, I want to tell him how proud I am!' Your
grandmother, a sensitive and very wise woman, succeeded in restraining him: 'Our son wishes to pray? Let
him pray; your presence there might embarrass him.' A
few days later I teased your father: 'So, Reuven, you're
going to become a rabbi?' He turned his face away as
he whispered: 'This is neither the time nor the place for
you to mock our faith.' And soon he began to haunt
places of prayer and study, singing and drama groups;
he began to live the life of a Jew in more ways than
one."

The two friends often took walks together, exchang-
ing ideas and impressions. Coming from widely different backgrounds, they reviewed and analyzed each
situation from various perspectives without ever reaching total agreement: what was certainty for one became

endless soul-searching and doubt for the other. They shared one preoccupation: how to spare the Jewish population not only the shame but also the persecution that caused it and to ensure, if not the survival, the safety of the greatest numbers possible, for as long as possible.

"Teach me," said my father, "give me vision and strength. From what point on and in what ways must my life change into an offering, into a sacrifice?"

"Our tradition forbids despair," answered the Rabbi. "Even as the sword touches your throat, turn your thoughts toward heaven: divine intervention is as quick as the blink of an eye."

"Shall I have the strength to hope, Rabbi?"

"Our Law, since Moses, is opposed to human sacrifice and suicide is just that," said the Rabbi. "Our Law, centered on life, is opposed to death, even when it is summoned for so-called lofty motives. To die in another man's place is forbidden."

They walked the streets of the ghetto where everything seemed unreal. Death was everywhere and timelessness clung desperately to the present. They walked greeting the passersby who gathered wherever some food was being distributed and all the while, the Rabbi was telling my father a controversial story about Rabbi Akiba and Ben P'tura. The two Talmudic sages had quarreled over the following problem: two men are walking in the desert; they are thirsty but all they have is one jug of water: enough for one man, not for two. What to do? Said Ben P'tura: let them share it; friendship is worth more than water, more than life. But Rabbi Akiba decreed: let the jug's owner drink the water and cross the desert and let him defeat death. Because, according to Rabbi Akiba, that is the Law: *Khayekha kodmin,* your life comes before any other life; though you may be able to save a life in

the desert you may not do so by sacrificing your own.
"I find this law shocking," said my father. "It lacks
generosity, compassion, brotherliness. I expected something else from our tradition."

"Let me explain," said the Rabbi. "*Khayekha kodmin*
simply means that your life is not your own. In other
words, friend, you are not free to dispose of it. That is
the basis of our tradition: one may not play with
another's life nor with one's own; one may not play
with death. And yet . . . there are times when we must
choose death over shame. Over abdication."

"Teach me," said my father.

Spring arrived in New York with a huge splash.
Rain, rain, rain. Specks of sun, ragged clouds, broken
sidewalks and roads. The crowds in the streets no longer
hurry, the schoolboys no longer play in the snow. One
more week and the last storms will be gone. One more
week and Central Park will be green.

"Speak, Bontchek."
I am cold, he is not. He drinks and that warms him. I
need to hear him talk to emerge from my lethargy.

We are sitting on a wet bench. Not far from us, nan-
nies are watching a group of children yelling in the di-
rection of another group of children who, for some
unknown reason, do not yell back.

Since our first encounter we spend much time together, Bontchek and I. I neglect my studies and my
friends. Never mind, they'll wait. There is no hurry,

only a need to know the past of this man who knows my
father's past.

"Tell me, Bontchek. The children, how did they live
in the ghetto? Did they laugh? Did they have fun?
What games did they play?"

I think of my childhood, I see it flash by, a flame is lit
and quickly goes out. Teachers' faces, teachers' voices:
"Come on, let's go, a little hard work never hurt anybody." Moses and Washington, Jeremiah and Lincoln,
Rabbi Akiba and Moby Dick, Mishna and algebra.
"Come on, young man, you're not paying attention."
Not so, I am paying attention. Sholem Aleichem and
Mark Twain. "Your parents work hard to pay for your
studies and you . . ." I know, I know. My father does
not spare himself, he is exhausted, he works, he works
from morning till night because tuition is expensive and
so is the clinic and so is life. I know. High school, college, exams, I know, I know.

"So, Bontchek, stop dreaming! Say something."

He takes another gulp from the bottle, just like a
bum, but we are not on the Bowery but in Central
Park, the largest, greenest park in the world, doesn't he
know that? Yes, Bontchek knows but doesn't care. Here
he goes again, evoking his memories; I was going to say
our memories. Why does his voice mesmerize me? Is it
the impact of his personality? My thirst for knowledge?
My need for a presence, perhaps? The city and its sea-
sons, the skyscrapers and their blinding reflections, life
and its childish pursuits reach me only through a muf-
fled and infinitely painful music.

"In my mind I see the ghetto and I still don't understand how I managed, how any of us managed, to endure its demands. When you entered it, you left the
twentieth century. All reasoning, all habits, all social
contracts with their advantages and constraints, all di-

plomas and titles were shed on the other side of the wall. For the first time in our history, knowledge and wealth became useless for the same reason: they no longer helped us, even to survive. Suddenly gripped by the unforeseen, you lived a life more real and yet less real than before: every hour could be the last, the sum of your existence. Listen, young man; even from a logistical point of view, what we were doing was slightly miraculous. In less than one week an entire community, that is to say an entire town, that is to say an entire world had to move and resettle. Families from vastly different social backgrounds suddenly found themselves thrown into the same building, what am I saying: into the same hovel. Do you know, young man, that a repugnant moldy hovel became home within a single morning? One soon became attached to it. Former homes: forgotten. Style, comfort: erased from memory. The children adapted themselves very quickly to the new rules that transformed the ghetto into a world of fantasy. We were living in a condensed time: people acquired instant habits. As soon as one arrived, one was a veteran. Strange: the structure and components of our centuries-old community were undergoing a radical change and yet, after the first tremors subsided, life once again became normal; men greeted one another in the street, women huddled in the kitchen, beggars begged, madmen sneered and history took its course."

Meanwhile, Richard Lander meticulously pursued his work. The deprivations worsened. The occupier's demands multiplied. Jews no longer had the right to own valuable objects, foreign currencies or jewelry. Communication with the outside was forbidden. Then they were required to enlist in the work brigades. Every

morning, they left the ghetto by the hundreds, heading
for the various workshops to repair railroad tracks, chop
wood in the forest, build barracks and stores, clean
kitchens and warehouses, maintain the workrooms and
offices of the military personnel. "Our goal is purely
educational," said the governor. "We shall teach you to
overcome your laziness. You have been perverted by
the Talmud; now you shall become useful at last, doing
concrete, necessary and important things!"

During his daily briefings to his colleagues, my father
did not try to hide his fears:

"We are trapped. To breathe, to live, we are forced to
compromise with the enemy who, we know, will use our
efforts to prevent us from living; more precisely: in
order to live, we shall help the enemy to kill us better.
But . . ."

The members of the Jewish Council of the Davarowsk Ghetto were accustomed to my father's ways.
They held their breath; there was always a "but."

"But what if we said 'no' right away? What if we answered that in this war, Germans and Jews cannot be
on the same side? What if we said plainly and firmly
that, at most, we concede the fact of their physical and
military superiority over us, but while they can force us
to work for them as individuals, they cannot force us to
make *others* work, meaning we shall not detail our
brothers to infamous tasks. . . ."

My father had expressed himself dispassionately, un-
emphatically. He had simply articulated the problem.
A lively discussion followed. Some extolled refusal and
opposition, others advocated feigned temporary submission. The Rabbi had the last word. Stroking his chin
as he often did when delivering his sermons, he said:
"When our ancestor Jacob prepared to confront his
enemy brother Esau, he had three options: bribery,

prayer or war. War is always the last measure to consider. Here, today, our lives are not in danger. Forced
labor? One doesn't usually die of it. On the contrary, it
will help us gain time, and that is what we need. Tomorrow we shall know more."

A mocking voice was heard:

"And prayer, Rabbi? What if we tried prayer?"

The council members looked around to identify the
insolent speaker. The Rabbi shielded his eyes with his
right hand and answered softly:

"Prayer? Yes indeed, why not? Only we don't have
much time. . . . And our prayers are slow."

My father insisted on only one tenet, that of equality
in the face of danger. At his suggestion, the members of
the Jewish Council were the first to volunteer for the
harshest of labors. They came home at night exhausted
but proud.

"You should have seen us," Bontchek continued, as
he wiped his mouth with the back of his hand, having
swallowed yet another mouthful. "You should have
seen us chopping wood. The director of the hospital, the
Rabbi, your father: the Germans shook with laughter
watching us. I was the youngest and strongest and the
best worker, to give you an idea. . . . It was a joke, but
what mattered was to make believe. To play the game.
After two or three days we had become experts. What I
mean is that there was no gain for the Germans, no
practical, concrete gain. Although now that I think of
it, they fooled us after all. They didn't want our work;
they wanted to humiliate us. Yes, it was a game. And
they were pulling the strings. They had us where they
wanted us: pretending, sinking into deception and
falsehood. . . .

"In any case, after one week, the *Angel* sent the council members back to their official duties. There followed a period, how shall I say, a rather idyllic period. Everybody seemed content. People said: it could be worse. Or else: with a little luck, we'll live to see the end of the war. I tried to organize a nucleus of resistance among my friends and comrades but found it impossible to convince them. They said: to resist is to endanger the life of the community. There were some, not many, who agreed to help me find routes leading out of the ghetto, out of the country, toward Palestine. Yes, young man, yours truly had succeeded in establishing contact with our friends abroad. And it was yours truly who accompanied the first group to Hungary and from there, to Romania. To the port of Constanza. I still remember the ship: a wreck of a fishing boat. As I remember the captain's bedraggled mustache, the crafty smile of the watchman whose palm we had greased. The weather was fine: July or August. The morning breeze. The noises of the harbor emerging from darkness. My friends' departure.

"There I stood on the wharf. I was cold. I was literally shivering with cold. What a fool I was! I could have left with the group; they had begged me to. There was among them a young girl—Hava—on whom I had a crush. Did she suspect it? Did she feel it? As we said good-bye, she drew me close and kissed me on the mouth. I thought my heart would fail, it was pounding so. 'Are you really not coming?' she asked. 'Do you really want to go back?' I was so stunned I didn't know what to say. My voice refused to obey; the words wouldn't leave my throat. And, sure enough, you want to know the truth? I felt like following her, never leaving her. Oh, yes, that's how I felt. But I was a fool. And naive to boot. I told myself that I was needed back in

Davarowsk, that the council counted on me, that your father could not do without me. And then too: I didn't believe things would turn out so badly. Nobody did. And so, there I was, back in the ghetto, chortling like some drunken hussar, telling your father all about my glorious adventures."

THE GHETTO of Davarowsk, I know it now. I find my
way around easily. My father's office, the Rabbi's clandestine *shtibel*, the official infirmary and the other, underground one, where serious cases and victims of
epidemics were treated. The ashen faces of the workers,
the empty eyes of the sick, I could describe them all. It's
as though I had lived there.

Bontchek is my inexhaustible guide and teacher. To
share his memories with me, he plunges back into them,
plucking from them here and there, a strange image, an
unreal scene, a fragment of life that will nourish my
imagination for nights on end.

I love to listen to his tales as much as he loves to tell
them, as much as he likes to drink. In my impatience I
sometimes taunt him a little: for example, if he dwells
too long on a detail I consider uninteresting or if, on the
other hand, he passes too quickly over an episode which
I suspect has a mysterious sequel. He then becomes annoyed and mutters: "Who's telling the story, you or
I? Who was there, you or I? Either you let me speak or
I'm going." Never mind, what's the use? I am at his

mercy; I am his prisoner; without him, my imagination will not be fueled.

From him I learn the end, not of the ghetto, but of my father's presidential career.

"One summer night, it is hot, we are playing with the stars, weaving dreams, basking in soothing nostalgia, as I said, one summer night, suddenly the earth begins to shake: your father summons us to an extraordinary session. Why extraordinary? Because. Your father loved that. For him, in those days, nothing was ordinary. A Jew was beaten and immediately the council was convened. A sick woman fainted in the street and your father immediately recorded the fact in the official chronicles of the ghetto. Your father hated routine. 'The day we shall treat a human tragedy, of any kind, like an ordinary event will be the day that marks the enemy's victory.' That is what your father told us over and over again. In other words, one more extraordinary session should not have startled us unduly. But that particular night, he was right. It was. . . . Listen carefully:

"A team of workers, some fifty men, had failed to return to the ghetto. Yanek, Avrasha-the-Redhead, the two clerks of the fruit and vegetable merchant Sruelson, a comrade of mine with whom I played cards on the nights I was on duty at the council: all good men who knew how to handle themselves. Had they vanished? Had they merely been delayed on the way? Transferred? It was the first time we faced such a disappearance: why lie to you, my boy, I was in a cold sweat. Somebody suggested sending a scout—but send him where? Into the forest, of course. To the workshop to which that team had been assigned. I had an idea: I knew a blond

girl, she could pass for a Pole or a German; she knew
the area. She was a member of my Youth Movement.
Not beautiful but gifted like a thousand devils or perhaps I should say like a thousand actors. She accepted
the mission. She slipped through the barbed wires, disappeared from sight and returned two hours later. She
had not seen anyone. By then it was eleven thirty at
night. No news was bad news. This business was becoming more than worrisome.

"In the meantime, of course, the families of the missing men had gathered at the council. 'What is going
on? Tell us, what is happening?' they were asking. And
wouldn't we have liked to be able to tell them. To
whom could we turn? Somebody, I believe it was the
Joint Committee representative, suddenly remarked:
'This morning I saw a group of SS. New guys. I wonder
whether they could have had something to do with . . .'
Your father, opposed to anything that could provoke
hysteria, interrupted him: 'What's the connection?
There is none.' All right, there was no connection. Still,
our fifty Jews had disappeared. And we, as members of
the council, were supposed to be informed.

"Someone suggested to your father that he contact
the authorities, more specifically, the *Angel*. At this late
hour? Why not; surely this was an extraordinarily urgent situation. Your father agreed. He lifted the re-
ceiver, dialed the number and introduced himself: This
is Dr. Reuven Tamiroff, president of the Jewish Council, who wishes to speak to . . . he did not complete his
sentence: at the other end someone had simply hung
up. Impassive, he redialed. An officious voice instructed
him not to disturb the Kommandantur so late; that he
could, if he so wished, call the next day. Someone asked
whether by chance your father knew the *Angel*'s private
number. No, he did not. What to do? Wait. All night?

And the next day, if need be. Nobody went home. Instead, our wives and children came to join us. Together we spent the night contemplating a thousand hypotheses, some optimistic, some pessimistic; together we scanned the darkness outside. The sky was starry and beautiful, so beautiful that one, no, that I was moved to consecrate a prayer to it. Why is the sky so blue, so deep, every time a tragedy is in the making?

"The stars went out at random, in groups, and then, wearily, one by one. Then it became dark, darker than before, darker than ever before, and then came sunrise more reddish and golden than ever before. The ghetto emerged from night almost reluctantly: what would this new day, heavy with foreboding, bring? Would we find the strength, the necessary incentive to live through the hours that were already recorded in an invisible registry, the one God uses to separate the living from the dead?

"Sitting with his head cupped in his hands, Rabbi Aharon-Asher recites in a broken voice the Bible passage that describes in detail the punishments and maledictions our people will endure if it succumbs to the temptation of transgressing the Law. 'At night, thou shalt pray for the morning to come and in the morning for night to fall . . .' Here is morning; it bears the seal of fate. Red turns into purple, the gold crumbles and becomes dust. Your father telephones the German authorities of the Kommandantur: 'Not here yet.' The governor takes his time; we wait. He won't be long. But he is delayed. 'Call back.' A few Jewish councillors rush to the ghetto gate. We question the people leaving: Yesterday, did they see anything? Anything unusual? Anything suspicious? Yesterday, did they happen to meet any of the missing workers? Not a single one? No. Some hours drag; others rush by nervously. At last, your father decides not to wait for the telephone. He has a permit to circulate in town; he presents it to the guards who return it to him without a word and motion him outside the gate.

"Once he is on the other side, he accelerates his pace, runs to the Kommandantur. The guards are expecting him; they accompany him to the governor's office. The *Angel* welcomes him graciously, invites him to sit down, apologizes for not having known that he was trying to reach him the previous evening: his act is perfect but your father is not in an appreciative mood. He is forced to do something he has never done before and which may cost him dearly. He cuts the *Angel* short: 'Fifty men have vanished as if swallowed by the earth; are the German authorities aware of that fact?' The governor, arms crossed over his chest, smiles amiably: 'But, of course, we are aware of it, it is our duty to know everything.' He uncrosses his arms and rests them on the desk: Oh, he is so sorry, the military governor is so sorry not to have thought of informing the president of the Jewish Council to reassure him. What a shame, but of course it is an omission, an oversight, he was going to do it, but the work, dear Mr. President, you know what that is like, the daily worries, the new problems, the war, you understand. . . . Your father requests information: where are they, these fifty men? Can they be reached? When will they be back? Are there any sick, any wounded among them?

"Don't forget, this is only the first phase of the ordeal: the enemy still wears many masks and we are gullible, we *want* to believe. When the *Angel* plays the part of benevolent protector, of defender of the Jewish worker 'who contributes as best he can to the war effort of the Third Reich,' we fall for it. And he is pulling out all the stops. He brings to bear his charm, his powers of persuasion to reassure your father. 'You mustn't worry, dear President,' he tells him, 'your Jews have been transferred, temporarily, I swear to you, entirely temporarily, to a new *Baustelle,* an important construction site where they will perform an urgent and rather secret task, you understand. . . . So don't worry. As soon as the project has been completed, they will return, I promise you, have I ever lied to you? They will be reunited with their families. Come now, Mr. President, stop frowning, they'll be home in a matter of days. . . .'

"Your father is not fooled; he senses that something is very wrong but he knows, too, that it is better not to let it show; he knows that above all one must never unmask a tyrant who believes he is a good liar, it is much too dangerous; as soon as he realizes he has been exposed, as soon as he knows that he is no longer believable, he becomes ferocious, cruel, deadly. 'Thank you, thank you very much,' says your father. He takes his leave and returns to the council. We hang on his every word: Well? What is going on? He is in no rush, your father. He can't make up his mind. He hasn't come to any conclusions. What will tomorrow be like? And the rest of us nervously, feverishly, try to read him, try to measure the density and significance of his silence.

" 'Come on, tell us . . .' Imperceptibly, he lowers his head as if to hide his gaze. 'Nothing,' he says, 'nothing precise, except . . .' We jump on him: 'What are you hiding from us?' Some get angry. 'I am at a loss,' he says. 'The *Angel* is friendly; he maintains that the fifty men are well, that they will come back, that we are imagining things. . . . But . . . I . . . have an odd premonition that troubles me.' We howl like madmen: 'Premonitions, you? Since when are you superstitious?' We bombard him with endless questions. Poor man, all he can do is shake his head. 'I don't know,' he says. . . . 'I only know one thing: I have a strange premonition. . . .'

"In the meantime, life goes on, it must. The work crews leave, the children go to school. Another ordinary day goes by. Two. Three. We think about the missing men but we no longer talk about them: such is the unwritten law of the ghetto. One does not discuss subjects that risk upsetting the balance; one does not mention anything capable of tearing down the veil of the future. Within a few hours we have settled into new habits. The missing men? Surely they will reappear one beautiful morning. Undoubtedly they are staying in another ghetto, possibly Kolomey or Kamenetz-Bokrotay; they will finish their work and be sent home. Patience. And above all: no panic. Only you see, my boy, things that are meant to happen, happen; it is not by looking the other way that we can change their course: if they must befall us, it is senseless to look away. . . .

"One night we learn the news and it is tragic, horrible: the fifty lost men have been found. On the other side of the woods. In a ravine. Shot. A bullet in the neck. A comrade of mine, a woodcutter, was the one who noticed something amiss. Close to the spot where he was working the soil had been disturbed; he went closer to investigate and slipped. The earth cracked open and when he fell, he found himself among the corpses. By chance, he was alone and therefore there was no panic. He came to see me that evening trembling like a leaf. 'You caught a cold,' I said. He didn't answer, he just kept looking at me, staring straight at me. We were in the office and people were beginning to watch us. 'Let's go out,' I said. My comrade followed me into the street. In the commotion outside, no one paid attention; one could talk. And he told me everything. I felt nausea well up inside me. I wanted to throw up. 'Are you sure you didn't dream this?' I asked. He

was sure. 'You didn't invent any of it?' He hadn't. If I
didn't believe him, he was ready to lead me to the site.
'No,' I told him, 'that is not necessary, not yet. Let's go
back to the council.' I took your father aside, I told him
that he would do well to call one of his extraordinary
sessions. Your father does not ask useless questions, he
knows me; I don't speak lightly. And then, he is not
averse to these sessions, I told you that. Besides, it
wasn't difficult to call a meeting; the council members
were always available, except for the Rabbi who sometimes went away to study, pray or teach; but everyone
knew where he was and in less than a minute he was
informed. Anyhow there we were in the meeting hall.
Your father gave me the floor. I mumbled: 'I'd like to
introduce a comrade of mine; listen to him.' We listened. Since Moses no Jew ever had such an attentive
audience. Eyes filled with tears, faces twisted, fell apart,
turned to stone.

"My comrade had stopped talking for some time but
we were still listening to him. What were we waiting
for? I don't know. We may have been waiting to hear
him retract it all, to hear him laugh and say: 'Good
people, I'm not finished with my report, listen to the
rest: the dead all rose from their graves and are preparing to come home tomorrow morning; it was all a
nightmare.' But no. The witness testified and fell silent;
he too was waiting. The hospital director was the first
to respond. 'I don't understand,' he said. Thanks, that's
terrific: he doesn't understand; what about me? What
about all of us? Did we understand maybe? Your father
commented: 'But why?' That's some question. Why,
what? The lies, the playacting? The murder of fifty
Jews? Our gullibility? Our illusions? Perhaps even our
complicity? Why, why? ... The Rabbi said: 'We shall
have to inform the next of kin; they shall have to

observe mourning.' That's what was on the Rabbi's
mind. Religion, rituals, God. I felt like saying something to him but thought better of it. He was a good
man, the Rabbi, I liked him and hurting his feelings
would surely not make me feel any better. 'But,' said
the Rabbi, 'first we must be absolutely certain.' Certain? Of what? That they were dead? 'What do you
mean?' I snapped. 'Is my comrade's testimony not
enough for you?' Yes, it was enough, but Jewish Law
requires the testimony of two people. He explained:
'Suppose a widow wishes to remarry, she must be able
to prove that . . .' Whereupon, despite the respect I
owed him and felt for him, I interrupted him and re-
minded him that this was not the proper time to give us
a lesson in Talmud. He was not angry with me, I know.
He was biting his lips, he was desolate, but so were we
all.

"Everyone was silent. A strange silence that buzzed
through the room like a swarm in the garden. Abruptly
your father turned to me: 'To ease my conscience, I still
would like to have a confirmation; what if you accompanied your friend?' It was not an order; hardly more
than a suggestion. How could I say no? 'All right, I'll
go.'

"My friend and I knew a secret passage out of the
ghetto, we left in silence; we entered the forest in silence; in silence we walked among the trees. Suddenly
my friend pulled my sleeve: 'It's over there.' We halted.
Again, the urge to vomit; this time I didn't hold back;
bracing myself against a pine tree I vomited. I vomited
my food, my insides, my childhood. I didn't want to
live anymore. I didn't want to breathe the foul air of
this earth. 'Come closer, look,' said my friend. I did as
he told me. I looked. I would have done better not to
look. . . .

"We started back and yet I felt that I had not left the mass grave: I continued to look, to stare at the bodies. We were back at the ghetto and I was seeing them still. We arrived at the council office and they were there too: tangled together but not disfigured, they seemed to be alive, to be living inside death. . . .

"The council was there, ready to listen to me. Two hours had passed since we left: nobody had moved or said a word. Motionless, riveted to silence, they were staring into the void in front of them and perhaps even inside them. Had they seen us return? I headed for my usual place, dropped into my chair but stood immediately. Why? Surely I sensed or knew that a witness must speak standing up. But . . . what could I say? Where was I to start?

"A thousand words jostled one another inside me; a thousand cries tore me apart. 'It's true,' I told them in a hoarse, unrecognizable voice, 'it's all true.' I knew that I had to go on, I knew that I had to say something else or perhaps the same thing differently, but once again I felt nausea. I was afraid I would throw up in front of everyone. And so I sat down again. I felt their eyes on me, searching, probing; they all wanted to see and not see what I had seen. If someone asks me a question, I shall get up and run away. No, I underestimated them. They asked no questions and I added nothing. How long did we remain like that: disoriented, disarmed, paralyzed? Until the first glow of dawn? Until the last?

"Your father looked at the Rabbi questioningly. The Rabbi said: 'I'm going to the *mikva*. Then we must prepare for the funeral.' Your father nodded his approval and said: 'What happened can happen again; tomorrow another group will have its turn. You may tell me that the special SS unit whose presence was tied to the

crime will leave our town or has already left; another
will succeed it. From all this I draw a conclusion: our
people must be told what has happened. If they refuse
to go on working for the Germans we must not try to
dissuade them. As far as we are concerned, one thing is
clear: the council must resign.'

"What followed then? Better ask: how did it end?
The news of the massacre plunged the ghetto into
mourning. There was shock, there was anger. The
ghetto was like a caldron under pressure, ready to explode. One cry, one wound, and there would be a revolt. Or suicide. The streets were filled with haggard
faces. Everyone was waiting for the inevitable decision.
What should we do, what could we do? Strangers spoke
to one another, pious women complained about not
being able to visit the cemetery outside the ghetto—to
alert the dead, to implore them to intercede up above.

"And at that moment, the barriers that enclosed our
forbidden quarter were lifted.

"Richard Lander arrived surrounded by his lieutenants. His face stern, flushed with indignation, the military man responsible for our fate hastened toward the
offices of the Jewish Council. Your father and the rest of
us stood waiting. He paused on the threshold: a kind of
border, a *no-man's-land* separating the two camps.
'What's going on?' said the governor without a word of
greeting. 'I am told that the brigades refuse to work;
may I know why, Mr. President of the Jewish Council?
Could it be that the war is over? That the Reich has already won? That we no longer need your efforts, your
talents? I have the right to expect from you, Mr. President, and from your colleagues, a more rational, more
sensible attitude. Your behavior distresses me as much
as it surprises me. Speak, I am listening.' Whereupon

your father, like a martyred king in one of those plays from antiquity, handed him a sheet of paper: our collective resignation.

"Richard Lander appeared to appreciate his adversary's role. If he was annoyed, he hid it well. His voice turned protective, warm, unctuous: 'Well now, why this refusal to serve your community, Mr. President? Is it because of the—eh—unfortunate incident that occurred in Workshop #4? To turn it into a drama would be a mistake, Mr. President. I do regret what happened. I regret it all the more because it could have been avoided. Would you like to know the facts . . . ? Four Jewish workers provoked the SS soldiers guarding them. There was a struggle, rifle shots were fired into the air. Convinced that they were under attack, the other members of the work force joined the mutiny. In their panic, our soldiers believed it necessary to shoot. Note that they were reprimanded and transferred. Does this explanation satisfy you? Will you now withdraw your resignation?'

"Everybody held his breath. I half-hoped your father would answer that he agreed to close the parentheses, and yet I would be lying if I denied having another reaction: the hope that your father would not allow himself to be duped by this wretched would-be actor. If he did, I would be ashamed of him; if he did, I myself would be ashamed in front of all my friends still staring at me out of that ditch, staring at me as if to tell me the story of their end, a story nobody will ever know. But, of course, my thoughts, my wishes were of little importance; the decision was your father's and it was sublime: he did not answer. I mean: he did not speak; he simply shook his head from left to right, from right to left, his jaw set, his eyes unblinking. He is strong, your father, and I admired him, we all admired him. Even those among us who would die and knew it, admired him.

"Sure enough, my boy, some of these men paid for it; paid for this gesture, this act of defiance, with their lives. The *Angel* dominated the stage and distributed the parts. He personified all the eternal powers and, as mercurial as they, made his decisions only at the last minute. But what would his decision be now? Until that moment I thought that, even for him, it was a game and that common sense would prevail. I thought: the ruler of life and death will say a few persuasive words, your father will answer with other words, and everyone will think that the match will continue, from ordeal to ordeal. . . . At what precise moment did I realize my mistake? Abruptly, the German officer drew himself up, stood at attention and declared dryly: 'You meant to give us a lesson in dignity—well, you didn't succeed. You see, Mr. President of the Jewish Council, we are German officers and our concept of honor differs from yours. Also be assured that we shall never agree to take lessons from you Jews, in this or any other matter.' Then I knew. Suddenly I knew that the end was imminent and inexorable. My stomach knew it, my fingers knew it. A shudder went through me; I was feverish.

"Pretending contrition, the German officer was now scribbling on sheets he tore from his notebook and then rolled into balls. 'I have here,' he said in a neutral voice, 'your twelve names in the palm of my hand. I shall throw away six, woe to them. They shall die.' And I found myself foolishly repeating the sentence: 'No he can't, he won't do this, not this, not now, not in this way, he wants to frighten us that's all, he is joking, it amuses him to see us panic.' Well, he was not joking. I remember what I felt: a sense of amputation, of absolute loss. To my right, Wolf Zeligson. To his, Tolka Friedman. To his, Rabbi Aharon-Asher. To his, Simha.

And then your father; I remember how changed he looked. A nervous twitch distorted his face. He made a visible effort to control it, to look straight ahead, to breathe normally.

"The *Angel*, who was observing us with contempt, turned to your father and said with feigned sincerity: 'You've drawn the good lot, Mr. President of the Jewish Council. I'm happy for you. All the more, because, for someone like you, and I know you better than you think, yours is the wrong lot. From now on, your future will smell of the grave.'

"And that was all. The end. In any case, the end of my association with your father. A new council replaced ours. The Germans were jubilant, their commander triumphant. The ghetto was shrinking. Here and there, the idea of organized armed resistance was beginning to take hold. Emissaries from Bialystok and Warsaw encouraged us: 'It's the only way,' they said. 'You must fight or die, you must fight until death.' I went underground. I escaped from the ghetto and returned bearing messages and sums of money sent by comrades near and far. Impeccable documents in hand, I traveled to places like Warsaw, Katowice and Lublin. Once I went to Vilna. My 'wife' on that mission was a particularly brave young woman. She was armed, I was not. I no longer saw your father. But he remained a presence in my mind. I could not detach myself from that last scene. But only much later did I remember a striking detail which did not concern him yet concerned us all: that night, the most astonishing and absurd night of my life, time, as if pursued by shame, had fled more swiftly: in less than twelve hours the Rabbi's black hair had turned completely white."

A

riel, my son,

. . . Daring? Honor? Dignity? What foolishness! To you I can admit it: I am angry with myself. I should not have defied our Angel, *not at that particular moment.*

After all, we, the council members, were not guilty of any wrongdoing as far as the community was concerned. We learned about the massacre only after it happened. We did not even know of the existence of Workshop # 4.

Then why did we insist on playing heroes? To obtain what favors in heaven or on earth? To impress whom? Now, in retrospect, I tell myself that to disarm the Angel *and blunt his rage, I should have thrown myself on the ground, crawled at his feet, and begged him to spare us. We could have resigned later. I could have told the Germans: "Before, we did not know, now we know; therefore, from now on we consider ourselves responsible for every life inside these walls. Next time a Jew is killed we shall denounce your crimes by resigning, by choosing death, next time . . ."*

Yes, my son, I feel responsible for the deaths of my comrades. Had I overcome my pride, they might have lived another year, another month, another day. For someone about to die even a single day is a long time. You know it well.

But . . . then what happened? I thought that I was interpreting our collective conviction that it was better, that it was simpler and more prudent to take a stand right then. Right there. Otherwise we ran the risk of falling into the trap of routine: one says B because one has said A. Then one continues to D, to death; one becomes an accomplice of Death.

I refused to say B. I stopped before. I was wrong. I could not resist the temptation of courage; that is how I sacrificed my friends. And others I didn't even know.

It is a fact that there were ghettos where Jewish leaders behaved differently; should I pity them or envy them?

I recognize that Jewish history placed too heavy a burden on my shoulders. I was not prepared.

Was the Angel right when he told me that I would have preferred to die? And give you up? Fortunately I was spared this choice. I was destined to lose either way.

Your father

H<small>E IS THREE TIMES</small> my age, Bontchek, but often it is I who support him. The strong and daring man who defied invincible powers speaks to me in a frightened and whining voice. He is convinced, Bontchek, that my father and Simha are ostracizing him, conspiring against him. I try to reassure him as best I can:

"You're imagining things, Bontchek. My father likes you, so does Simha. You're going through a paranoid phase, you suspect the whole world. . . ."

He shakes his head. He knows. My father and Simha have rejected him; they hate him. They exclude him from their debates because, in their eyes, he has done something wrong.

"We were so close," he cries, "so close. Like brothers. You cannot imagine all the wild, outlandish plans we watched take root and die, all the misfortunes we endured. Together we fought. Together, side by side. We formed a bloc. The German army, at the time the most powerful in the world, could neither break nor separate us. Now that the danger has passed, they turn their backs on me."

"You exaggerate, Bontchek. Admit that you're exag-

gerating. You say these things because they don't invite
you to their scholarly evenings. I didn't know you were
such a lover of Biblical studies."

"Don't you, too, make fun of me. They insult me, do
you want to do the same?"

"Really, Bontchek . . ."

"You think I'm paranoid? Then how do you explain
their conspiracy?"

"It is they who are inexplicable, Bontchek. They are
strange, you of all people should know that."

"In the old days, in Davarowsk, they were my
friends; they no longer are. Now they are . . . they are
my judges."

Poor old Bontchek: he would give all his worldly
goods—and mine—to rejoin his old comrades: to re-
capture his youth.

We meet more and more frequently. Endless walks.
Riverside Drive, along the Hudson River. Broadway
with its noisy, crowded cafeterias. And near the tip of
Manhattan, the Brooklyn Bridge, which we cross on
foot. Sometimes we venture into the subway, that dirty
foul-smelling labyrinth where everyone seems ill,
gloomy or conniving under the cold lights. The trains
arrive and depart with shattering noise, without ap-
parent destination. Sleeping workmen, widows in
mourning, leering vagabonds, teenagers on the run,
abandoned fathers bent under the weight of their solitude, prostitutes in quest of clients, civil servants playing hooky, thieves awaiting their opportunities, hungry
beggars, homeless children: what wretchedness, Lord,
what wretchedness Thou hidest from Thine eyes. . . .

During these outings I am the guide. Even though,
for the voyage into the past, I follow him. Strange jux-
taposition you will tell me: New York and Davarowsk.
And yet there is a connection between these two worlds,

believe me; the very same that exists between Bontchek and myself. Our goals are similar and overlap:
both of us attempt, through the other, to come closer to
my father. Bontchek conjures up the past and, in return, I describe the present to him: my father's obsession with One-Eyed Paritus; the half-romantic,
half-kabbalistic plans of Simha who hopes to restore
creation to its primary light by manipulating his faithful shadows; our silent vigils, our visits to our neighbor
Rabbi Zvi-Hersh, my sleepless nights, my migraines,
my confusion about my role within the family.

"You know my father. He is a complicated man. He
has lived many lives and now he tries laboriously to
build a bridge between them: who is the bridge? I? His
writings? His silence?"

"Why in God's name can't he be like everyone else?"

"He's not like everyone else."

"He could at least make an effort, couldn't he?"

"Why?"

"How should I know. To please me. . . ."

Bontchek is depressed. I ask him to return to the
ghetto, he refuses. He does not feel like chatting. To
change his mood, I tell him of my studies, my lectures,
my discoveries, my inexperience. . . . Lisa dragging me
to a party at the house of one of her friends. Everyone is
drinking and yelling, then they stop and begin to smoke
and listen to records. They hand me a lighted joint, I
refuse politely, they insist, Lisa insists. O.K., I inhale: it
is sickeningly sweet. My stomach is turning. I run outside, I vomit my guts, I go home, I feel robbed. Lisa's
comment: "It's your mother's fault." "What's my
mother's fault?" "Your weakness, your nausea . . ." As
far as she is concerned, it is always my mother's fault.

Why not my father's? Because she is very fond of him.
"Lisa has met him?" asks Bontchek, surprised.
"Yes."
"Tell me."

"One day she asked to meet my parents: 'But why,
Lisa?' 'Why not?' I tried to change the subject, to stall:
with her all such tricks were doomed to failure. Obsti-
nately, stubbornly, she insisted. And so I told her the
truth: she could not meet my parents because my
mother was in a clinic and because my father, since her
departure, tolerated no female presence at home. 'You
won't ask him to meet me? Fine, I'll go without an invitation.' 'Don't do it, Lisa. . . . Let me smooth the way.'
That evening I mentioned her to my father. His attitude surprised me: 'You care about this girl?' 'I . . . I
don't know.' 'And if I see her, you'll know? In that case,
let her come. Let her come tomorrow.' Besides, he
added, it had been a long time since he had had the opportunity to have an interesting conversation with a
young woman of my generation. Fine.

"Lisa and I arrived together the following day. Father greeted us smiling. The table was set: tea, pastries,
fruit. 'Your name is Lisa,' he said to her, shaking her
hand. He repeated: 'Lisa, Lisa.' And she answered that
yes in fact that was her name. With the help of her
sharp sense of humor, she overcame the malaise that
hovered over the living room. She reminisced about her
childhood—about the first time she realized that her
name and she were one, the origins of her first name,
her father's family roots. She teased me about my
shyness with the other girls in class. 'Do you know that
your son almost got a *terribly* bad mark in logic because
he was so intimidated by the professor he could not

utter a coherent sentence? You see, the professor of
logic is Annette Bergman, and she drives all the boys
crazy. . . .' Lisa stayed three hours. She was already at
the door when my father, squeezing her hand with
great warmth, said to her: 'So your name is Lisa.' He
had closed the circle by saying the same thing, and he
had said nothing else.

"That's all very well," says Bontchek. "Still your father likes Lisa whereas he shuns and excludes me. What
could I have done to deserve this?"

"You're on the wrong track, believe me. My father
tends to keep his distance from people. He is reserved.
But that does not mean that he is against you or anyone
else."

Bontchek is not to be convinced. He is obsessed by
the coldness he senses in my father.

"Is it because I used to chase girls? Because I was always ready for a fight, always eager to make a deal? Is
he reproaching me—still—for my dissolute past? My
escapades?"

"You're being silly. And unfair. Try to understand:
my father likes solitude and silence; in fact that is why
he chose to become a librarian."

One day, in the library, I had seen him with a
young-looking woman whose bearing and sensuality I
have never forgotten: just thinking about her does
something to me. Her dark hair fell freely over her
shoulders; her sensuous lips spelled invitation and desire. There she stood in front of my father's desk, asking
his opinion on Charles Ketter's posthumous poems; he
advised: "Read the early ones, reread the last." She
leaned over to look at the work he was studying:
"Paritus? Who is he?" "A one-eyed man who meditated
in exile." Oddly this provoked her: "Will you have dinner with me? I'm hungry." I was shocked by my father's

icy response: "We are in a sanctuary, madam, not on a cruise ship." She dissolved into tears and so did I. I was ten. I never saw her again. And now as I think of it, I realize that I miss her, have been missing her for a long time: no doubt I am more sociable than my father.

"You don't understand, you no longer understand my father," I tell Bontchek again. "Even I find myself excluded by his silence. Evidently he prefers his ghosts to the living. He may even consider himself a ghost. Have you seen him walk along the street? He floats, he glides, he threads his way among the passersby without ever brushing against them. Does he love death? I don't think so. But he loves the dead. He'll love me when I'm dead. You, too, Bontchek, he'll love you when you're dead."

Since Bontchek says nothing, I continue:

"Perhaps you think I'm too hard on him. I probably am. And yet I do love him. My love for him is total. But not blinding. He hides behind his eyelids, he shuts me out of his past. Let's face it, Bontchek, without your help, I would have learned nothing about what he endured in the Davarowsk ghetto. He doesn't answer my questions. Does he even hear them? I want to know, I tell him. The beginning of a story, the vestiges of a memory, I want to know what you knew about life, the world, the mystery of life, I want to know what you experienced in the company of human beasts who claimed history and God as their own; I want to understand, I want to understand you. Nothing doing: he stares at me, his gaze becomes darker and darker and he becomes more and more agitated; he sets his jaw, swallows his saliva and says nothing. He neither wishes nor is able to confide in me.

"Oh, I know: you'll tell me that all sons have prob-

lems with their fathers. The generation gap and other
such nonsense. But it's not the same. The things my father could tell me, no man will reveal to his son. Yet all
I want is his trust.

"I remember: one Friday evening we were alone and
I became angry. I lost my temper. I became disrespect-
ful. Why? It was fashionable to be ashamed of one's
parents at that time, toward the end of the sixties. The
country was upside down, embroiled in a massive up-
heaval. A blinding wrath had descended upon my generation. We didn't speak, we shouted. We loved
violently, we loved violence.

"We had just finished the *Shabbat* meal and my father
wanted to know whether I was staying home. In fact, I
had no plans to go out. But I felt the need to lie:

" 'No, I'm expected somewhere.'

" 'Who would expect you on a Friday night? You
know I like to have you here.'

"I don't know why but I exploded:

" 'You want me to be here? But why? To honor me
with your silence? Do you think it's fun to see you
gloomy all the time?'

"I don't know what got into me but I couldn't control myself.

" 'You claim to be a good Jew, you observe the laws
of *Shabbat,* you claim to be my father, but isn't it a father's duty to pass on his knowledge, his experience to
his son? Am I not your son, your only son? What kind of
father are you if you persist in living sealed off behind a
wall?'

"And to hurt him even more, I shot out this impu-
dent remark:

" 'No wonder we're alone tonight and every night.
My mother, my poor mother, clearly it is you who
made her sick!'

"My father opened his eyes wide and closed them immediately; he was breathing hard. Was it the reflection
of the candles on the table? His face suddenly looked
yellow and red, crossed with deep shadows. My heart
heavy and my mind in turmoil, I left him to go nowhere. I had offended him. Wounded him. Ask his for-
giveness? Dazed with grief and remorse I wandered
through Brooklyn feeling excommunicated. The songs
wafting out of the lighted homes, the joy they expressed, seemed to repudiate me, to condemn me to
shame and contempt. I recalled the Biblical law: a son
who insults his father deserves the supreme punishment. Why had I done it? To avenge my mother? To
conform to the spirit of the times? How could I make
up for what I had done? Had I turned on my heels and
gone home, had I thrown myself into my father's arms
to cry with him or for him, I could have fixed everything. But something stopped me from doing that. I
think I wanted to feel guilty, I wanted to go to the end
of my guilt, and every moment compounded my error
and increased my uneasiness. Why? In order to suffer,
of course. I made him suffer so as to suffer more myself."

I said it before: like my contemporaries I was going
through a crisis. One that had nothing to do with my
personal life. My generation was undergoing profound
crises; we had become painfully conscious of society's

ills on an international scale. Student uprisings in Paris
and other capitals of Europe were analyzed and reana-
lyzed on every campus. Something like a nausea of epi-
demic proportions was driving thousands of young
people to repudiate gods and idols living or dead. Yes,
nausea is the word that best describes the feeling that
drove my comrades, those I knew and the others, of that
period. Ideas and ideals, slogans and principles, old and
rigid theories and systems: everything that was linked
to the past, we rejected scornfully. Suddenly parents
were afraid of their children, teachers of their students.
In the movies, it was the criminal not the cop who won
our sympathy. In philosophy, the least important subject was . . . philosophy. In literature, negation of style
was in style. Morality, humanism were funny words. It
was enough to pronounce the word 'soul' to send your
listeners into paroxysms of laughter. Sometimes Lisa
and I would visit friends: there was drinking, un-
dressing, lovemaking while reciting the *Bhagavadgita*, a
mingling of obscenity and prayer, generosity and cruelty, and all this in the name of protest and so-called
revolutionary change. It was pure chaos. The young
wished to appear older, the old to remain young; the
girls dressed as boys, the boys paraded as savages. "If
this continues," I said to Lisa, "the Messiah will refuse to come." She made a gesture of disdain: "The
Messiah? Who is that? Do you think that I should
make his acquaintance?" To her way of thinking he
had to be a madman, therefore, someone she wanted
to meet.

Lisa was active in the radical Left and tried hard to
involve me. I was treated to huge rallies, fiery rhetoric,

demonstrations involving socially oppressed people, the deprived, the wretched, the ethnic and sexual minorities. The battle was in Vietnam but the front line cut across the campus. The present was being disfigured, but we were challenging the past, unmasking political machinations, denouncing authority. The university no longer taught literature or sociology but revolution or counterrevolution and even countercounterrevolution of the Right or the Left or in between. The students no longer knew how to construct a sentence, formulate a thought, and were proud of it. If a professor happened to voice his displeasure, he was boycotted, perhaps even told to go back to his scholarly works, his archaic ideas. Next time, he had better make sure to be born into another society, another era.

It would be foolish to deny the influence Lisa had on me. She was Rosa Luxemburg, the Pasionaria, my own Joan of Arc; she was leading the masses on to the barricades. Watching her in action I loved her even more. I vaguely felt that this movement of revolt she had made her own brought me closer to my father's memories, to the victims' dead memories. It wasn't clear to me how. I wasn't able to think it through, but I didn't care. I thought: So what, I'll think about it some other time. Indeed, other priorities had emerged: the march on Washington, the demonstration in front of the White House. And Lisa, my number one priority. I loved Lisa and Lisa loved political strife: the typical modern couple. Was my father pleased? If so, he didn't show it. But neither did he say he wasn't. While campuses were burning and institutions were tottering, my father sank deeper and deeper into his meditation on Paritus. Mankind was racing to destruction, the nuclear cloud was stretching to the horizon, but he went on analyzing

sentences that only seven times seven people, himself
included, would ever read.

It was Lisa, too, who introduced me to acid. At first I
resisted. I gave in only when she found a way to link the
drug to . . . my father. Nothing complicated about that:
she linked everything to my parents!

"You go on a 'trip' and you are free, liberated," she
said. "Free of your father, of your father as of everything else. Isn't that what you're trying to accomplish?"

"Maybe, I'm not so sure. I am less concerned with
freeing myself of my father than with freeing him. He is
the one you should convince to take LSD."

Never mind, she would have to find a better argument. As always when faced with a complicated problem she sat down on the floor, crossed her legs and
thought out loud:

"No thanks. Even if he says yes, all he will remember
in the end is that my name is Lisa. It's you I want.
Come with me. You won't regret it, I promise. Are you
afraid?"

"Frankly, yes. I don't drink, I don't smoke. And
you'd like me to take LSD just like that? Don't waste
your time. . . ."

"You don't understand," she pleaded. "You suck on
a lump of sugar and you succeed in transcending yourself; you become other, you attain the celestial heights
of the beyond. In one hour you become the equal of
Buddha, of Moses. And you, you'll go higher than they
ever went. Come on, what do you have to lose? Your
earthly ties? Your security? Come with me and you will
dominate the unknown, you will come out of yourself,
you will *be* yourself, come. . . ."

Suddenly I had an idea: in the course of the trip I might be able to get closer to my father; I might *see* his invisible universe, I might *live* his fear of death, I might *live* his death. What he had withheld from me in words I would find in images, I would see with my soul. .... I agreed.

"On one condition," I said. "I'll do it once. After that, no more. Will you promise not to insist?"

She promised.

"I'm not worried," she said, laughing. "You'll like it. You'll ask for more."

"We'll see."

The trip was set for the following week, in her tiny new studio in the Village. In the meantime I did some research. Three books a day on the subject: usage, effects and dangers. My father was surprised to see me, night after night, bring home from the library books on hallucinogens.

"Are you doing work on the subject?"

"Yes. For my psychology professor."

"I see."

And after a slight hesitation:

"You won't let yourself be tempted. ..."

"Don't worry, Father."

The dreaded and anticipated evening finally arrived. Lisa, gentle and solemn, gave me her instructions on how to prepare myself: Relax, let yourself go. Fly. Jump.

First, I conjured up my friend Bontchek. I recalled his stories of the ghetto. And abruptly, drawn by an irresistible force, I am far away, a very small boy at my father's side. Miserable. Confronting a starving, terrified mob. And, inexplicably, I am two people at once: I look at a trembling child and I am that child. I snuggle against my grandfather but at the same time I seek refuge in the crook of my father's arm. I feel like crying and not crying, howling and being quiet, running away and remaining still, I want to be and to cease to be, I see myself double and not at all, very tiny and terribly old and I ache, I ache, I feel my heart bursting with fear and happiness, yes happiness at being able to feel such pain, I feel my body becoming one with the body of creation and my mind becoming one with that of the creator, I feel every parcel of the earth, every fiber of my body, every cell of my being and they all oppress me they are so heavy, they are so light, and they all pull me skyward while pushing me downward, is that why my tears start to flow? Is that why I am speaking to them, calling them, drawing them close to penetrate me as a flame penetrates darkness? I hurt, the pain is overwhelming, and yet I don't care because I know that it is from and for my father, that it is because of him that, all of a sudden, I feel the need to hide, to huddle over there in the corner of my room, in the bend of the planet, that it is because of him also that I am shrinking more and more until I am small, smaller, reviving the child in me, even dying in his stead in the void, in the black and scorching nothingness. . . .

"You scared me," said Lisa. "You shouted, you wept. You begged Death to desist. And Life to illuminate the world. You said things, things that are not like you: you were not you."

Exhausted, breathless, I was coming back slowly, painfully, to my alternately numb and outrageously stimulated senses. My father, I thought. But my father had remained silent. Even in my hallucinated vision I had been unable to make him speak. I had spoken for him, but he had said nothing.

Suddenly I thought of Bontchek. Soon after their reunion my father began exhibiting surprising signs of nervousness with regard to his former comrade. Surprising because for him that is rare. Even when he is tormented or anxious, he will not let it show; even when he is angry, his eyes are not. Why was he so rude to Bontchek?

I remember the scene clearly: we are in the living room and Bontchek who is visiting our home for the first time is enjoying his slivovitz sip by sip. As I watch him I think to myself: strange character; a mixture of martyr and hedonist. A black, really black face as though covered with soot, flattened nose, powerful neck, square chest, he looks like a boxing coach or a fugitive from the Foreign Legion. But as soon as he opens his mouth, he communicates tenderness.

Clandestine journeys and struggles, the establishment of networks, adventures in the underground, the aftermath of World War II, Palestine, Israel and its wars: he tries to summarize the years in a few hours.

He seems to be trying to please or to justify himself. My father listens to him, amiably, attentively; he's clearly glad to see him again. The complicity between them is obvious. As always when I am in the presence of two beings whose relationship is genuine I am moved. I tell myself: "These two friends have known the unspeakable; one day they will begin to testify and will continue to the end of time." In my imagination I see the Messiah whom Simha has brought; I see Him approaching on tiptoe so as not to disturb us.

Suddenly I become aware of a change: my father is surreptitiously glancing at the clock on the wall oppo-

site the window. He is becoming impatient: this is the
last Thursday of the month, Simha will soon be arriving for their regular session. It is past seven; it is getting
late. How is my father going to extricate himself from
this rather delicate reunion? In fact, why would he not
invite his former comrade to stay? Bontchek knows
Simha, who will be glad to see him again. I am about to
make that suggestion, but my father reads my mind
and throws me a disapproving glance. Fine, I'll be
quiet. The minutes grow longer, the seconds stretch
under the weight of boredom. Bontchek, somewhat
drunk, somewhat incoherent, is in the process of attack-
ing two German tanks on a road near Bokrotay, my paternal grandfather's village. It is eight o'clock, the
problem becomes serious, dramatic, a source of tension.

I personally find Bontchek's tales fascinating. But
my father rises to his feet and holds out his hand to his
former comrade. "I am interrupting you, please forgive
me. I am expecting someone. Will you come to see us
again? I do hope so." Stunned, Bontchek stands up and
allows himself to be led, almost pushed to the door. He
is gone before I can say good-bye to him. I am troubled:
my father, discourteous? Rude to a companion from his
youth? To a refugee? I don't understand. I ask him to
explain: "Why couldn't he stay? Simha would have
been pleased to see him again, I'm sure of it!" My father's face is closed: "The subject Simha and I have
been studying for years is not one I consider appropriate for an outsider." His tone, as he says these words, is
surprisingly harsh. Could there be an unresolved con-
flict between him and Bontchek? A latent animosity?

That evening after Simha's arrival, my father takes
from his pocket an article he has clipped from an Israeli
daily; an eyewitness account of a confrontation between
an Israeli intelligence officer and a captured Palestin-

ian. Strangely, I remember it as though I had seen it on
the stage.

In a narrow office, somewhere not far from Tel
Aviv, three men are staring at each other: for them
the moment of truth, as they say, has come; they
must either cross the threshold or back away. In
either case the risk is serious, irreversible. What
means must they use to make the prisoner next
door talk?

That is the nightmare of every honest police-
man, as of every person of integrity: where lies the
permissible limit of force? How far may one push
violence before becoming dehumanized oneself?

The prisoner is Tallal, a twenty-two-year-old
native of Jaffa, who was captured in Galilee. Out-
numbered by the Israeli soldiers, he had surren-
dered immediately. He had no chance to escape
and knew it. Arms above his head, he waited for
his captors to come closer. He watched silently as
they relieved him of his Kalashnikov, his grenades
and his cartridges.

Brought to Military Intelligence headquarters,
he is subjected to a routine interrogation: Where
does he come from? Which camp? By what route,
looking for what trail? Who are his accomplices?
His local contacts? What exactly is his mission?
The questions rain on him and he remains mute. A
sergeant threatens him—to no effect. Another jos-
tles him somewhat roughly. Tallal shrugs his
shoulders and says nothing. Finally it is Ilan,
wearing a uniform which does not reveal his high
rank, who takes over:

"Listen to me, Tallal. My name is Ilan. I am an
officer. It is my duty to fight you and to render you
harmless. You and your comrades. Until now,
none of them has resisted very long; do you intend
to be the first? Is that it?"

Tallal is seated. His is an ascetic face covered
with a several-day-old beard. He leans forward as
if to see the officer better. They are alone. An ordinary desk separates them. Outside, night is with-
drawing toward the sea.

"Come on, Tallal," says Ilan. "What are you
trying to do? Make an impression on me and my
friends? Or on yours? Do you think you're stronger
and smarter than all of us? Why don't you speak?

"You do know that if we want to, we can make
you talk, don't you? Sure you know. Every nation
has its methods, we have ours. Believe me: you
won't hold out forty-eight hours."

Ilan is playing with a pipe he has just pulled
from an inside pocket; he stuffs it, stuffs it, he will
never finish stuffing it, but he will not light it; he
uses it to distract Tallal. There is something on the
Palestinian's mind. This is no ordinary terrorist.
The secrets he carries probably have nothing to do
with routine sabotage or intelligence operations; he
seems too sure of himself, too confident of being
able to resist torture.

"Make no mistake, Tallal. You won't hold out
forty-eight hours. Not even twenty-four. By the
way, neither would I. I am human, vulnerable just
like you. There is a suffering beyond endurance.
Tallal: all of us would do anything to avoid it. And
so it comes down to this: if we don't want to die we
talk. And since you will not die—we'll see to that, I
assure you—you will talk. That's right, Tallal,
you'll talk, you'll give in and you'll sell us your
comrades-in-arms, your friends, your brothers, and
you will be right: I too would rather face death
than torture. But ..."

Ilan pauses to check whether his pipe is properly
stuffed, and obliquely examines his prisoner.
Tense, watchful, Ilan can almost hear the blood
pulsating in the young Arab's temples. He is sur-

prised: he expected to discover relief, even hope on his face because of the "but." Oddly, Tallal's face shows only disappointment. Because he fears psychological torture more than physical pain? Because he suspects a trap? What is he hiding? In any event, Ilan sees a breach, one that needs to be widened.

"Don't worry, Tallal, you shall not be tortured. Though I've found torture effective, I also find it repugnant. I don't believe in it. It is my conviction that your weakness protects you. I can't see myself torturing a defenseless man. Anyway, why should I? Whatever you know, I know too or will learn soon from other sources. I don't care to dirty my hands, to lower myself in my own eyes. And so . . ."

He strikes a match and blows it out at once:

"Let me tell you what I plan to do with you: you'll stay in prison, you'll be brought to trial and—because you were armed—the military tribunal will condemn you to life imprisonment. Not so terrible. Tomorrow there will be peace between our countries. You will end up going home."

Now Ilan is convinced: the thought, the prospect of not suffering worries the terrorist. Yet he does not appear stupid. Ilan doesn't understand, but he hides his irritation. Then, he sees a shudder quick as lightning go through the prisoner. It lasts only a fraction of a second but Ilan notices. What is he so afraid of if it is not suffering? And suddenly, the answer is obvious: he wants to suffer. He has prepared himself for suffering, for torture, probably for death. The reason? Perhaps to set an example. To lengthen the list of Palestinian martyrs. To feed anti-Israeli propaganda. And also to force the Jewish adversary to practice torture, therefore, to betray himself, therefore, to choose inhumanity. For Ilan, it is a dilemma. . . .

My father is excited. As he puts down the article he keeps repeating: "For Ilan, it is a dilemma." Why is his voice trembling as he asks his friend's opinion? His elbows propped on the table, Simha mumbles his answer:

"I don't see the dilemma. If Ilan thinks what he says, then Tallal's silence represents no threat and he should not submit him to torture."

"But how is one to know? How can one be sure? What if Tallal is more cunning than Ilan and it is all a ruse; what if he has an accomplice in prison, a plan, a strategy: in that case, would Ilan not be better off to use every means to make him confess?"

"Then . . . you are for torture?"

"No," my father says firmly. "I am against. I am opposed to it in theory and in practice. Torture dehumanizes both torturer and victim."

"But . . . you are not against capital punishment?"

"Yes I am. And so are you, Simha. What is the point of all our studies here if not to restate and confirm our opposition to the ultimate humiliation: death inflicted on man by his fellowman?"

"His fellowman? That's going a bit far."

"In the eyes of Death that is what all men are," says my father. "The problem is the moment, frozen in time, that precedes Death and which represents man in his totality."

Whereupon my father launches into a disquisition on morality and phenomenology, alternately quoting Parmenides and Heidegger, Hegel and Hüsserl: time and perception, language and names and their infinite connections illuminated by consciousness. . . . In the end Simha must interrupt him to bring him back to the subject:

"Nevertheless, Ilan is facing a dilemma: Tallal alive

represents a definite danger; dead, a possible danger. Surely the state must assume its responsibilities: to disarm Tallal without killing him, to render him harmless without striking him. So far, there is nothing that cannot be resolved. But let me go on, let us imagine, if you will, since imagination is a component of torture, let us imagine that Tallal knows that a bomb will explode the next day and cause the death of many human beings; let us imagine that Ilan knows that Tallal knows. A Tallal of superior intelligence determined to turn Ilan into a torturer could definitely force him into that position. What would Ilan do? If Tallal is permitted to remain silent, it spells disaster. How can one make him talk?"

"By setting traps for him," says my father. "If Ilan is good, he will trick him into speaking; if he's not, he should be replaced."

"And what if tricks don't work? What if there is not enough time? Intelligence, psychology, ruse require time, it could take hours, days. There is only one shortcut in this domain: torture."

"I'm against it," my father insists.

"What do you propose instead?"

"Ilan is the one who must propose something, not we."

"You tell him to act, then you judge him, that's too easy."

My father almost chokes with indignation.

"That's not true and you know it, Simha. I let him act and I judge myself."

The discussion—stormy, absurd—continues until late into the night. Dazed with fatigue I force myself to keep my eyes open. Curiosity keeps me awake: what would I have done in Ilan's place? In the morning, at breakfast, I ask my father how the evening ended.

"Nothing justifies torture," he says.

A disturbing thought crosses my mind: what would I have done in Ilan's place?

"What about death?"

"Nothing justifies death," says my father.

I find myself in perfect agreement with him but I still cannot understand why Bontchek was not allowed to take part in the discussion.

ON THE EVE of the Jewish New Year I take the bus to Pokiato, a sleepy little town in the shadow of the Catskill Mountains. I have so much on my mind that I do not read the newspaper I bought at Grand Central Station. I have never taken this trip without anxiety. At the other end lies naked and unconscious pain.

My mother.

She lives in Pokiato. Anyway, she resides there. The clinic is well maintained. Clean. Superb comfort and medical care. Delicious food. Television and games under the supervision of an unusually competent and caring staff. End of commercial.

My mother.

Each time a little smaller, a little more peaceful. Inside her darkness whom is she calling? Her eyes, a faded blue, see without seeing, glide over me without lingering, without letting me in.

People help her to get dressed, to lie down, to walk, to eat. They call her and encourage her, they scold her gently, they lecture her, they urge her to behave.

I send the nurses away. I want to be alone with her. To speak with her. Perhaps, with a little luck, to make her speak. To pierce the veil, crack the wall, make her feel my presence, my need to learn her secret.

I stroke her hands, they are still as slender and delicate and smooth as those of a child; I run my hand through her hair tied into a chignon; I touch her forehead, her sunken cheeks, her eyelids. And I speak to her and speak to her.

A ray of sunlight enters stealthily and is reflected in her eyes. I jump: is it a sign? I fall back disappointed. Still, I tell her, we must not give in. We must not lose hope. Tomorrow evening is the beginning of the New Year celebration. I shall pray for her. I shall pray for all of us. For the living and for the dead. Pray that the dead, appeased at last, cease tormenting the living.

All these words, did I really say them? My mother did not hear them. Since the age of six I have been speaking to her and she does not hear me.

When I place myself in front of her, as I do now before leaving her, when I lean over her, she looks at me but she does not see me. When she finally does see me, whom does she see?

On the way home Simha sits beside me, more somber than ever. I didn't know it, but he too comes every year to visit my mother before or during the High Holy Days. When we met at the bus station, we both smiled, embarrassed. I don't feel like small talk. Neither does he. That's good. The bus is moving at breakneck speed. The highway: relentlessly straight, bordered by billboards. A cloudless sky. I let my thoughts wander and enter the ghetto where Simha's presence is more real to me than on this bus. The forbidden and condemned quarter has become my home; I know its early morning sounds and its nocturnal rustling of wings. The moan-

ing of the dying, the mournful chanting of the gravediggers, the dead orphans' litanies: I hear them all.

Suddenly, in a low and stifled voice, Simha begins to
tell me a story of that time, the story of an event that
was to be decisive in my father's life and his own and
which illuminated facets of their personalities that were
new to me.

"Your father and I are bound by a kinship that has
withstood the years and their upheavals. We have always been on the same side. Even when Rabbi Aharon-
Asher pronounced himself against a particular action
your father supported, I stood by him. Do you know
what I mean? No? Still, you should be able to make a
good guess: you are often at our monthly reunions. We
are forever seeking arguments to justify ... an act, a
grave and terrible act that we committed together, long
ago. . . ."

AUTUMN 1942. With the New Year, the ghetto of Davarowsk sinks into misery and despair. The sick die, the elderly fade away and disappear. The ghetto laments: "Hear, O Lord, receive our requests, inscribe us in the Book of Life." The military governor Richard Lander, usurping the Lord's role, decides who shall live and who shall die and in what way. On the Day of Atonement, the holiest day of the year, he organizes a manhunt: "Thus, the Jews shall have proof that their God has chosen to remain deaf to their prayers."

In the early morning hours, two hundred men and women have already been herded into the ghetto's only square. It is a beautiful day. The sun is generous with its favors. A grayish smoke seeps from a chimney somewhere inside the Christian town. A silence born out of the hollow depths of time envelops the condemned and isolates them from the living. "It is today that the decree is signed up above: the fate of men and nations has been determined: who shall win and who shall lose, who shall eat and who shall go hungry, who shall die of plague, and who of suffocation . . ." Surrounding the two hundred, the Jews of the ghetto of Davarowsk

recite the solemn prayers. Here and there you can hear
people sobbing.

For the moment nothing happens. The *Angel* inspects
the ranks, directing a friendly word to an old grandmother, another to a crippled war veteran. He stops in
front of Fischel-the-Furrier and questions him:

"You don't look well. Are you sick? Oh, how stupid
of me! You are fasting, isn't that it? Or am I wrong?"

"No, sir, you're not wrong. Today is a day on which
we are forbidden to eat, drink, wash . . ."

". . . and make love," continues the *Angel.* "You see? I
know your laws by heart."

The standing, the fasting, the thirst, the uncertainty,
the fear: here and there a man collapses. Exhausted, a
woman cries out, is quickly silenced, and begins to weep
softly, her husband whispers into her ear just as the
Angel begins to speak.

"Ladies and gentlemen!"

The crowd leans forward as one. The *Angel* clears his
throat.

"I thank you for your attention. I have a favor to ask
of you. I like Jewish prayers. It would please me to hear
you recite them. And even more, to hear you sing
them."

The people can't believe their ears. They think he is
mad. To pray. To sing. Here? Now?

"You seem surprised; that troubles me, I must tell
you. Aren't you Jews? Isn't today Yom Kippur? What
would you do if you were in synagogue? Imagine that
you are at services. And then . . ."

He pauses a moment, inhales before continuing:

". . . also imagine that I am the Lord your God."

All around him, hundreds and hundreds of men and
women, and children too, watch, not daring to breathe.

"I have time," says the SS officer. "One of God's attributes: He knows how to wait. Like Him, I have infinite patience."

He withdraws to the shade and sits down on a stool. He lights a cigarette, leafs through the newspaper, chats with his subordinates as if the Jews no longer existed.

In the sky a silvery cloud stretches gracefully, its vapor fading as it enfolds a flock of birds. A man faints while following them with his eyes.

"Well?" asks the *Angel*. "What about those prayers? Carried away by the birds?"

Nobody moves. The officer goes back to reading his newspaper. An hour goes by. Normally, at services, the morning prayer would be over by now and the *Mussaf* would have begun.

Suddenly a woman comes forward:

"Mr. Officer," she begins.

He stands up and faces her:

"Who are you?"

"Hanna. My name is Hanna Zeligson. I am Simha Zeligson's wife."

"I'm listening. You want me to hear your supplications? You want to recite your prayers to me? Go ahead, let's hear you."

She straightens up, stands there erect and dignified, dusting an imaginary speck off her dress.

"I can't," she says at last.

Her voice is clear though a little weak.

"You can't sing? Nor pray? Then why . . . ?"

"I can sing. And I know how to pray, sir. The women here are educated. We attend services and know how to read Scripture. But . . . I *cannot* do it. Not here."

The officer appraises her:

"Why not? I just told you: imagine that I am your Lord, your God!"

"That's just it, sir: you're not."

"I don't understand your scruples," says the *Angel* after a brief silence. "I thought that Jews like to pray; you spend your life praying; in fact, you have traversed History praying all the while. . . ."

"Indeed, sir," says Hanna Zeligson still calm, head held high. "For a Jew to pray is an affirmation of faith only when it is freely made. It is up to us to choose the object—or subject—of our faith. Faith in God, yes; faith in our ancestors, yes again. Faith in Death, never."

The officer takes a step forward as if to strike her, but he changes his mind. The actor in him has the upper hand.

"I am not telling you to pray to Death but to God. And what if I told you that Death is God? Listen to me, Jewess: my voice is the voice of your death. Cover it with prayers and perhaps you shall live."

"Never," says Hanna Zeligson.

"It will be your own doing."

He bows courteously and departs. His subordinates are kneeling, ready to shoot. The dazed crowd waits in silence. From time to time a body falls. The sun at its zenith turns heavy, leaden. Here and there a man or a woman staggers. Others appear to doze standing up. As if under a spell, they all try not to think of the reddening sky, of the burning ground. Who shall live, who shall die? The two hundred shall die. Before the day is over, before the *Neila* service is ended, all will have perished.

Standing tall over the corpses, defying heaven and earth, SS officer Richard Lander is shouting:

"You see, I was right to proclaim it: I am Death and I am your God."

That same night, four men meet in an underground shelter: Reuven Tamiroff, Simha Zeligson, Tolka

Friedman and Rabbi Aharon-Asher. Still fasting. In
the dim light they all look pale, sickly.

"I invite you to take an oath," says Reuven Tamiroff,
coming straight to the point. "Whoever among us shall
survive this ordeal swears on his honor and on the sanc-
tity of our memory to do all he can to kill the killer,
even at the cost of his life."

"We swear it," reply Simha and Tolka.

"And you, Rabbi?"

"First, I'd like to speak to you, my friend Reuven."

They withdraw to a corner crawling with spiders,
cobwebs all over them. Simha watches as they argue
without rancor, never raising their voices, never taking
their eyes off each other. The Rabbi defends Jewish
tradition and Jewish Law which prohibit murder; Reuven pleads for the victims. "How can you defend the
executioner, Rabbi?" "It's not the executioner I'm de-
fending, but the Law. The Law must not be broken,
Reuven. The military governor is an assassin, everybody knows that; he must be punished, I agree with
that. But wait until he has been judged." "*We have*
judged him. Look upon our group as a tribunal." "A
tribunal? Composed of only four members? Twenty-
three are required. Moreover, the accused is entitled to
a defender, did you forget?" They leave one another at
midnight, each clinging to his position.

"This was the first time they disagreed," said Simha.
"Also the last."

For me, it is a breakthrough. Suddenly I understand
a great many things.

A*riel,*

I know: you won't believe me, you will be shocked, perhaps even disappointed, terrified, but it's the truth. It is important to me that you learn this: your father has actually shed blood, he has committed the ultimate violence. I have killed, Ariel. I have destroyed a life. It is because of the dead, because of you, my son, that I have killed. To vindicate you I have assumed the role and mission of avenger.

The man I executed or helped execute is someone you knew and who knew you: Richard Lander, the military governor of the ghetto and town of Davarowsk. The Angel. *You do remember him, I'm sure. He remembered you.*

We condemned him to death. The trial was held in due form. I was a member of the tribunal. And also of the group that carried out the verdict.

I shall tell you everything, my son. You have the right to know. And besides, you are aware of it all. Where you are, only truth matters, nothing else exists.

Listen, Ariel.

April 1946. Your mother and I, miraculously saved in separate camps, belong to the tribe of the wanderers. Even when we stay in one place, we are nomads; our heads and hearts are searching for other places far away, nonexistent places to find rest.

I shall not tell you of our experience in those camps for survivors; they are not readily described. The daily humiliations. The constant depressions. The recurring feeling of being "superfluous." No country will have us. No visas. Draconian quota restrictions. Debasing medical examinations. We are treated as slaves or beasts of burden. The rich nations admit only the rich; that is to say, the relatives of the rich, the physically sound, the young. As for the elderly, the sick, the desperate, the emotionally crippled, let them stay in the barracks while the international rescue organizations strain to keep their bodies and souls together.

As I said, it is 1946. We are in a "Displaced Persons" center near Ferenwald. Bleak days, nightmarish nights. I am not myself: I know it's irrational, I know it's illogical and childish but I go on looking for you, I look for you everywhere, constantly. Not like your mother: poor thing, she has found you. She sees you. She speaks to you. She tends you and feeds you. She never tires of praising your beauty, your precociousness. At first, I make an effort, I say: "You mustn't, Rachel. You are sinning against nature. And against the Almighty." Then I give up.

One day, Simha pays me a visit. We embrace. He lives in Belsen. I watch him anxiously: could he be searching for his wife Hanna? No, he saw her die, all of us saw her die. He is looking for me. To bring me up to date.

We find an empty corner so that Simha may speak confidentially. It has to do with the Angel: he is alive.

"Yes," repeats Simha. "He is alive. We have picked up his trail."

Do you know, Ariel, that words can strike like objects? Do you know that they can cause pain?

Simha elaborates: it was an officer of the Palestine Jewish Brigade, whose secret unit tracks and punishes the worst of the

Nazi killers, who discovered the executioner of the Davarowsk Ghetto.

"The Angel has been spotted in a provincial town called Reshastadt," says Simha. "Our friends are keeping him under total surveillance. Do you . . . ?"

I can guess his question.

"My answer is yes. We have taken an oath. What right do I have to betray it?"

I don't need to go into details, my son. Simha and I left for Frankfurt where our friends from the special unit gave us our instructions for the following week. I'll describe them to you another day. What matters is that the operation succeeded. Our friends were professionals. Preparation, execution; in truth, Simha and I were but assistants, extras. It was they who chose the place and the time; it was they who threw the grenade. As through a thick mist, as through the walls of a distant ghetto, I saw and heard the explosion. I saw a man—the Angel—slumped on the pavement. Mission accomplished. Ambulance, police cars. This is 1946; occupied Germany barely functions. The death of one man neither shocks nor rouses indignation. Just another news item. . . .

Later we talk about it often, Simha and I, during our regular monthly reunions. Would I have taken part in the operation had you not been involved? Was I right to participate? We both rummage for ideas and precedents to justify our deed retroactively.

Nothing but words, Ariel, I know. Justice has been done? One makes that claim, one is wrong to make that claim lightly. Even if one could execute the Angel a thousand times, six million times, justice would not be done: the dead are dead, my son, and the killer's death will not bring them back.

I think of my friend Rabbi Aharon-Asher who, from the beginning, spoke out against our methods. And what if he was right?

Your father

FATHER," I say hoarsely. "Who is Ariel?"

He seems weary, my father. As always, since I can remember. I know I should spare him, leave him alone, but I cannot. I am so tense it hurts. I beg him to speak, to explain: what I have just discovered threatens to upset my universe. It would be absurd not to pursue it.

"I am not a child anymore," I continue. "Stop protecting me. I feel the evil forces prowling around us; I want to know them."

I am on fire: I can feel the flame running through my veins. I hear a voice—my voice?—saying:

"You have spent years writing letters to someone you call Ariel: who is he? You call him son. Is it me? Who am I, Father?"

He shifts uncomfortably in his chair as if it were burning his skin, he stands up, sits down, rises again, opens a drawer and closes it, moves toward the window and comes back.

"I didn't think you knew," he says weakly. "These letters, where did you find them?"

"By chance. One day I wanted to read your manuscript on Paritus. They were hidden inside. . . ."

He avoids my gaze. Clearly, he feels guilty. I cannot imagine for what.

"And so you've read everything?"

"No. Not everything."

"The story of the oath?"

"Yes."

"How did it affect you to know that your father once took part in an execution?"

"It didn't."

"Don't tell me it leaves you indifferent!"

Indifferent is a strong word, but not entirely incorrect. Stories of vengeance have never thrilled me. Sure, I applaud the Nazi hunters, especially those of the Israeli Secret Services, who track down war criminals the likes of Eichmann and Mengele, but to reduce the Event to that seems simplistic. My father, in 1946, punished an assassin? Fine. In those days, that was undoubtedly the thing to do. What stood out was the name Ariel. My father writes to him with a tenderness that troubles me; I must find out who he is.

"So be it," says my father.

He takes the manuscript and pulls out several pages and hands them to me. I stand and read.

Outside it is dark. Inside it is dark. A thick, tightly pressed crowd is waiting for the gates to open to see the sky and breathe fresh air.

The mood is somber. There is an awesome finality to the event. We are old people without a future. Our resignation removes us from this world. Why were we marked for this first convoy to "the East"?

A child's voice—yours, Ariel?—brings tears to my eyes. What luck, we are together. Yes, that is the word I heard: luck.

*I answer: we are going on a trip together. I love trains, says the
child.*

*As for me, it is not the trains I like; it is the railroad stations.
I could spend days and days in them without getting bored; I
could watch my life unfold surrounded by travelers rushing about
oblivious of me. Only railroad stations too have changed. Too
large. Too modern. The electric trains: too shiny, too efficient, too
clean. I prefer steam locomotives. The hissing, the whistling, the
white smoke.*

*You must have been six years old, perhaps a little more, when
we were in a station for the first time. It was a small one, I remember. And old, I remember that too. A very long, very dark
structure opening onto the platforms. People crying, that's normal. Soon the train will pull in, there will be separation. Take
it easy. Someone says: take it easy. It is useless. People shove,
knock against each other, step on each other's toes. Insults,
prayers, knowing glances. Lord, have pity on us. Someone says:
Lord, have pity on us. A madwoman answers laughing and I
don't know what she said; I only know that she laughed. Voices
are raised: make her shut up, oh, yes, she should not be laughing,
not here, not now.*

*Then suddenly it's evening. The gates open and a man in uni-
form—very tall, very strong: a giant—comes to inform us that
the train has been delayed; it won't arrive until tomorrow. A good
sign, somebody says. A bad sign, his neighbor answers. How
shall we spend the night here? a voice asks. There is no room to
lie down. Never mind, we'll take turns sleeping. Not the children, says an old man, and I shall always remember his voice
though not his face. The children will sleep in a corner near the
open window. Wrong. The giant orders the windows shut. A
woman shouts: but we'll suffocate! Others join in: we'll suffocate, we'll suffocate! All right. The giant is kindhearted; two
small skylights will remain open but it is forbidden to go near
them. Understand? No, I do not understand, not yet; that night*

you left us, you were six years old; you are still six years old.
Dead children are lucky; they don't grow up.

My father is distraught. He mumbles a few sentences
and every word is a stab. Once upon a time, once upon
a time there lived a little Jewish boy named Ariel, Ariel.
. . . That little boy, that little Jewish boy was endowed
with every gift, with every grace. . . . Ariel was the favorite, the spoiled child of the ghetto of Davarowsk. . . .
Ariel was the glory and future of the doomed Jewish
community of Davarowsk. . . . Anyone ready to drift
into hopelessness had but to see him smile to regain
courage. . . . Ariel was the heart Rabbi Nahman of
Bratzlav speaks of—the heart of the world, the heart
that resembles a human being yearning for love and
beauty. . . .

I listen to my father and I have the feeling of hearing
an ancient tale I knew long ago but had forgotten. The
words flow and fuse into one another and it seems that
he is repeating himself over and over as if to cast a spell
over me. From now on I shall understand many things
but I don't know whether that will be a source of pain
or comfort. My father's solitude and the more visible,
more concrete solitude of my sick mother: both living
with their dead child; both seeking in me their lost son,
my brother Ariel.

Where am I in this dream?

I am overcome by sadness. I am falling into a well, I
think I can hear the sound my consciousness makes as it
hits bottom.

So as not to succumb entirely, I reach out to my father. What I feel for him at this moment is more than
love; it is something else. I would so like to protect him,

to give him back his youth, his vigor, his capacity for happiness, his authority over me, his life.

"Ariel, my little Ariel," he says whispering like a guilty, unhappy child.

"Yes, Father," I say.

His eyes cloud over, his breathing becomes heavier as he repeats:

"Ariel."

"Yes, Father."

He stiffens for a moment, then he lets go. He bursts into tears, he who has never wept. For whom is he crying? For his dead son or for the other who has usurped his place?

I feel crushed by the weight of the past.

To counteract my obsession with Ariel I invent another: the *Angel*. I need to learn more about him. I run from one library to the other, from one documentation center to the other. I consult *The New York Times* archives, I ask Lisa, who is going to Washington, to consult the special archives of the Library of Congress, I write to the historians Trunk and Wulf, and gradually I find clues: the character becomes less blurred, less elusive, he slowly takes shape.

His name is mentioned four times at the Nuremberg trials. His activities are described at the trials in Frankfurt where the executioners of Auschwitz were judged. Witnesses report having seen him in Belzec and Chelmno, places he had visited to perfect his training.

I even succeed in finding a photo. It shows him in SS uniform, whip in hand, making a speech to a group of officers somewhere in Poland. I had discovered the photo in a little-known album entitled *Images of Death*.

A reference to his theatrical ambitions can be found in the deposition of SS Colonel von Gleiwitz whose extradition to Poland in early 1952 aroused cries of outrage in the German press:

". . . in Davarowsk we were faced with a rather ridiculous problem: after the day's work, my men of *Einsatzkommando II* were forced to listen to the endless discourses of the local commander, a certain Richard Lander, an SS lieutenant colonel and, on occasion, a decidedly mediocre actor."

Holed up in my tiny student's room, swamped by papers, I ask myself: who am I? What am I to do with a life that is not mine, with a death stolen from me by my own brother?

Late at night I sometimes worry about my sanity. I am alone and yet I hear voices, Simha's and Bontchek's tales. Lisa suspects me of taking drugs: I look, she tells me, like a dying man.

How am I to overcome the desire to let everything go and give in to my voracious nocturnal ghosts?

My relationship with my father has changed: I find it more difficult than ever to speak to him, for I do not trust him. On the other hand, my ties to Bontchek and Simha have become more precious to me; I meet them separately. I talk to them. I make them talk. I complain about my father, they defend him. Lisa wants me to marry her. "You cannot marry a dead man, Lisa!" I tell her.

My work goes badly, I have a hard time concentrating. Metaphysics now bores me as much as medieval poetry: the killer of Davarowsk has taken possession of me, impossible to get rid of him.

I stand up, I sit down; I open a book and close it; I go out only to come back a minute later; I scribble notes which I throw into the wastebasket. And my exams are approaching. A paper due on Freud and mythology. Another on Wittgenstein. A third on the theme of "origins" in Eastern thought. . . . My head is bursting: names, theories, formulas that call for similarities or differences in concept, attitude, intuition. I must forget the people inhabiting me, the faces that obscure my vision; I must also forget, totally forget, Richard Lander or I shall never earn my degree. My hatred for this Nazi killer grows; even in death he pursues me with his wrath, his whims, his desires. Yes, even in death he will not let go of me, he drives me into that forbidden zone where there is no distinction between prayer and blasphemy, between triumph and defeat, between life and death; he pushes me toward chaos, toward madness. And the more he pushes me, the more the distance between us diminishes; the more he reveals himself, the more engrossed I become. I am tracking him down and yet I am his prisoner. For such is the life of the survivor. . . .

Then one day, incredibly, there was the *Angel*. I made my sensational discovery in May, six months after my talk with my father, in *The New York Times*. Though dressed in civilian clothes, he nonetheless looked vaguely familiar: the studied concentration, the controlled gaze, the hint of a supercilious smile. . . . More than the people around him, he moved on an invisible stage. I seized a magnifying glass, studied the photograph, rushed to my files, feverishly pulled out the album, let the whole thing spill out of my hands, but the coincidence was blinding: it definitely was the *Angel* looking at me from the pages of *The Times*. Under an assumed name—Wolfgang Berger—he currently held an enviable position in German and European industry. His name appeared in the article in connection with a medal conferred on him by a philanthropic organization.

Holding my head in my hands I try to think. I find it difficult; my brain has ceased to function. The end . . . I feel I have reached the end. Drained. Broken. I should be laughing, laughing as I have never laughed before. But I cannot. Instead, I am overwhelmed by a lethargy that will soon paralyze me. I think of Bontchek, Simha, my father and I try to imagine Ariel. I talk to them: "So you didn't know, did you, that the *Angel* is a philanthropist, a friend of mankind?" As in the old days under the influence of LSD, I huddle in a corner of my room, but sadness, like an evil wind, chases me. With what is left of my energy I grab the telephone and call Lisa: "He is . . . alive." She does not understand. I repeat to her the most extraordinary news in the world and she still does not understand. She thinks that I am ill, overwrought, that possibly I have lost my mind. Still she drops everything and jumps into a taxi. "Would you like me to tell your father?" "Oh, no, Lisa, please! Not a word to my father!"

I wonder about my father. He is capable of ruining this too, just as he ruined everything till now. I pity him: that is the feeling that suddenly dominates all others. How can one be so clumsy? He killed a man and it was the wrong one. Inexperience or bad luck? Fact is he missed. Anyone, even a fool, is capable of inflicting death: not he. He and his friends, avengers? What a joke! Faced with a professional they can't hold their own. Poor Father, you're nothing but an amateur. The *Angel* is not dead the way our dead are dead, he is not even dead the way we are; he is alive and mocking all of us as usual; he is winning, as he always did. To know how to kill, one must love Death. He loved it, you did not. He was Death's accomplice while you were only its victim or, at best, its adversary. And, poor Father, don't you know that it is not man but Death who kills? By killing, the killer celebrates Death! The *Angel* knew how to go about it; Death and he were on the same side; whereas you knew nothing. And now? Now it is too late. You know it well, Father: whenever man wonders: "And now?" it is already too late. And where do I fit into all this? Too late for me as well. For me, for you. Since I am not your real son, are you still my real father?

Poor Father. You bungled the attack as you bungled the rest. You endured the universe as one would an illness and life itself as one would a failure. Paritus is not your mentor and his meditations are of little interest: you chose the wrong idol as you chose the wrong prey. Better to have left both to oblivion. You failed the test. You failed the ancient glory of Davarowsk.

Lisa, always practical, takes over and calls the whole world: the State Department, the librarians in Washington, Harvard, Chicago, Yale and Reshastadt, asks questions in every imaginable language, implores and demands, cajoles and howls until she joins me, exhausted, on the floor.

"All right," she announces. "I know everything. Wolfgang Berger or, if you prefer, Richard Lander, was lucky: the wound was only superficial. A scratch ..."

She laughs, I cover her mouth with my hand: this is not the time.

"You must admit it's funny," she protests.

Her levity irritates me. A rich kid amused by the misfortune of others. I am filled with resentment— doesn't she understand anything?

"No, Lisa. It's not funny."

"Then what is it?"

"Sad. Profoundly sad."

"Sadness can be funny . . ."

"Stop!"

She does not persist. I continue:

"The one time that Jews react like anyone else, they are incapable of carrying out their mission! The one time they choose action over meditation, they fail! It's not funny, it's pathetic."

We decide to go and tell my father and his accomplice Simha. No more remorse! No more penance! They have suffered for nothing! All their investigations and all their studies for nothing! All their guilt: also for nothing! It is our duty to tell them.

When he sees us arrive, my father becomes anxious: could something have happened to my mother? We try to reassure him but we don't succeed. I ask him to call Simha: "Now? Right away?" "Yes, it's urgent." He obeys: Simha will be here soon, at nightfall.

I show them the photographs, they take their time examining them. Lisa gives them her report. My father is in a state; he does not stop muttering: unbelievable, unbelievable. Simha, emerging from his shadows, is rubbing his chin: impossible, impossible. In the bleak light of the living room they remind me of scolded children; they scarcely dare lift their heads. Impossible? Unbelievable? That's what you are. . . . What foolishness to believe that in this society, justice could be done by the victims of injustice; what an idea to want to write History in terms of ethics and generosity. How naive can one be? Go call your third crony, that nice Bontchek, go ahead, invite him to your useless, childish meetings, go on, the game is over.

I leave them in the living room. Lisa and I run down
the stairs. In front of the Lubavitch House, the crowd
heaves forward to enter and listen to the Rabbi singing
with his faithful. Three streets down, a church is drawing hundreds of blacks. On the avenue, there are addicts
sprawled on the sidewalk, sleeping a troubled sleep.

We go to my apartment. Lisa is radiant. We are in
love. At least one certainty.

The next day I feel better. I resume my studies. I
write my papers. May ends with a success. I get my
diploma. Good-bye, City College, good-bye, experts in
phenomenology. Bontchek, would you like a drink?
Another one? No, no: don't start your tales again, I've
had my fill of them! Simha, give me a present: smile,
yes, come on, leave your shadows, you will not go to hell
for a crime nobody committed, shake yourself, my great
kabbalist: look for God in joy, He's there too, I promise
you. What if we went on vacation, Lisa? To the mountains, perhaps? What do you say? I love the mountains.
You prefer the seashore? Very well, let's find a sea in
the mountains, shall we? Long live summer, long live
peace!

Except that summer lasts only one summer. Return
to New York. Unbearable heat wave. Gloomy father.
It's contagious. Leave him for good? I cannot. I don't
want to. In spite of everything and because of everything, I love my father, notwithstanding all those who
like to hate theirs. Close the parentheses. I fall back into
my routine, but I do need a job.

It would be so easy to pretend, to go on "as if." So
easy? Maybe not. In truth it is impossible to pretend.
And it is a good thing that it is impossible, otherwise
life, stripped of memory and meaning, would lack all

warmth. To change events, to mold the imagination, to seize panic at the source, desire at its birth: all this is possible only when one does not pretend. You, Ariel, you give me pause, you make me wonder: I refuse to act and go on "as if."

During September I write a lot. More than before, more than ever. To relax? To understand. To reconcile myself with my father. I follow his example: I write letters to Ariel. If he can write to his lost son, then I can write to my lost brother.

M*y dear Ariel,*

I see you more clearly than I see myself; do you know that I miss you? Nothing would please me more than to be your big brother and guide you through tunnels strewn with treasures and to defend you against any wild beasts that might be lurking in the dark; nothing would please me more than to play with you.

Now close your eyes, try to close them, so as not to see us. Listen to yourself become silent, peaceful, hold back those screams that rise within you. Try to rest, Ariel. Ask for nothing, look for nothing. Try to accept, try not to make it worse. It is in your power—at last—to allow yourself respite.

There is peace in you; your eyes once looked innocently around you, your hands once felt the sweetness of a caress, your heart once fluttered anxiously. Let it become memory, not suffering: today's deprivation does not mean that peace and gratitude do not exist. For Father's sake, for mine, try to transform the peace of the past into a new peace, a necessary peace. Rekindle in your eyes your first vision of life, of your mother, our mother; of the sun, of trees; of shadows called Simha or Bontchek or Ariel; we must live and die with such visions for a deliberately empty gaze brings only more nothingness.

Simha and his shadows, Bontchek and his drinking, Father and his silences: look upon them with trust, give them your innocence or rather your thirst for innocence. Give them what passed for your childhood, or, better yet, give them what remains of your childhood.

Do not reject others. Accept yourself for yourself, for me. I imagine your face, beautiful and shining and troubled. Bow down, never mind if you get dizzy. And never mind if your tears flow. Be true to yourself, Ariel. Let your gaze come to rest. Stay like that. Your gaze; it contains all the intensity, the sum of what came before, before the exile. Here, there is only weakness and that is why man must find in these glimmers, in these signs, the strength to confront his destiny. Do you know that to join two words requires as much power as to join two beings?

Now you must sleep. You are weary, exhausted, as I am. Try to sleep in spite of it all, try to gather some strength for tomorrow. If for no other reason than that an image of peace, however awkward, however faltering, is seeking to follow you into the reality of death: a child runs in the forest and he runs without fear and he shouts because that is what he feels like doing, and he calls me because he likes me, that is the image; it isn't much but I have no other.

You must close your eyes once more and be still and try to rest; don't listen to me, listen to your desire to sleep; I am that desire. Listen to your past which is also, in more than one way, my past. And weep, let your tears flow, go on, let them, and then try to retrieve a smile, the first smile on your mother's, our sick mother's grief-stricken face.

Your brother

September 20

Ariel, little brother,

Don't be angry with me, but I am irresistibly drawn to Germany. I think I must go there. The position I have found in a university will wait. I wish to see the site, the place where our father attempted the irreducible act on your behalf. The urge to follow in his footsteps has become overpowering.

I imagine that this seems strange to you. It has been weeks since I've thought about the ghetto, the screams, the killers. I felt I had reached a harbor from which no blood-stained shore was visible. I was wrong. It suddenly came over me again, last night. I had dinner with our father. Simha was there too, explaining the theme of anger in Jewish mysticism: there was, he said, a celestial, a divine blessing called Anger. Suddenly he paused, let his head drop to his chest, as is his habit before speaking in a personal, intimate tone, and continued: What would the sea be without the waves that whip her? What would life be without the anger that shakes it? And God, what would His creation be without Death, what would love be without hate?

When I got home, I called Lisa; there was no answer. I thought over what Simha had said and realized that hate was one of the things that I had managed to elude, and suddenly I didn't know whether to be proud of it or not.

In truth, I am drawn to hate. I am drawn to the Angel. I need to hate, to hate him. I look upon hate as a solution for the present: it blinds, it intoxicates; in short it keeps one distracted.

It occupies my mind: and what if our father was right? In

that case it would be my duty to complete his unfinished work, to correct his mistake, to succeed where he failed.

And so I have decided to fly to Reshastadt. To reopen the file. To reenact the fateful instant in time. It would be cowardly to shirk my obligation using the pretexts of legal prohibitions or the years that have elapsed. As long as the Angel and killers of his kind exist, the spirit of man will remain flawed. They have killed eternity in man; they have no right to happiness. By depriving you of a future they committed unspeakable crimes: not to remind them of what they have done would be an insult to you. If Richard Lander is happy it means that happiness is forever corrupt. If the Angel can sleep peacefully somewhere, it means that the world has ceased to be a haven and has become a jail.

Your brother

September 21, 3 a.m.

My little Ariel,

I am too excited, I am afraid I shall not sleep. I took a sleeping pill. I was dozing off when the telephone rang; Lisa wanted to come by. I said no, not now, tomorrow perhaps, I need to be alone. She didn't insist. She hung up and I was grateful. Ten minutes later, there she was ringing my doorbell: your voice sounded sick, she told me. It has happened before: she knows when I need love.

A sick voice: is that true? A sick mind perhaps. A sick imagination. Otherwise why would I be going to Germany? Don't tell me it is to recover.

Your brother

September 25

Ariel,

*I envy you, little brother. They took you when you were small;
you took your childhood along like a toy. Pure, whole. They have
not sullied your life, my little brother.*

*For me, you see, things are more difficult. There are tempta-
tions that are too difficult to overcome and even more so to ignore.
Such as to fulfill one's life through suffering. Or Evil. Since
Good leads to Evil, why not reject it from the start? The mystics
of ancient times were confronted by this seemingly insoluble
problem: the Messiah, they said, will appear the day that all of
mankind will be either just or unjust. In that case, why not try
injustice?*

*I don't say this for myself. I am too weak. Too vulnerable. If I
cause suffering I suffer twice as much.*

*I say this for those who are the incarnation of Evil. For those
who have torn you from life, my little brother. Is it possible that
their crime was part of some divinely incomprehensible plan? I
consider the hypothesis and I am embarrassed; it is as if I were
trying to comprehend the men who delivered you into the flames;
it is as if I were trying to put myself in their place when, with
all my soul, I yearn to be in yours.*

*I envy you, Ariel: you are in your realm, yours alone. You are,
whereas I am becoming.*

Your brother

ALL SORTS of tormenting thoughts race through my feverish brain as I settle into the empty compartment. As usual I am too early, since I constantly worry about being late: a mishap, an accident, a memory lapse, an obstacle, anything is possible. Result: I wait and grow impatient and am annoyed with all those horrid people who appear on time.

What am I looking for in Frankfurt? What am I going to do in Reshastadt? Reason would dictate that I take my little suitcase and go home. Take a trip with Lisa. Run with her in the sand, climb mountains, and sleep, yes sleep.

I am tired: the plane landed late. Then I walked to kill time. My legs feel weak. I have not closed my eyes all night. I shall sleep on the train.

I love trains. I prefer them to planes where, for an exorbitant sum, you travel wedged between a compulsive talker and a neurotic dinosaur. At least on a train you have the option to get up and stretch your legs in the corridors; you open the window, you breathe the fresh mountain air and if you so desire, you can always count and recount telegraph poles, cows, sheep, whereas the view from your little porthole in the plane, let's not talk about it. Blue, nothing but infinite blue; such bad taste, it's enough to make you sick. Maybe if I were in a hurry, but I'm not.

Well now, it is raining over Frankfurt. Just as it did long ago.

Long ago, my father took the same train, probably at the same hour, for security reasons: a train ticket is like an arrow in the dark, it leaves no trace. Instinctively I glance over to the platform: have I been followed? I reason with myself: don't be silly, you haven't done anything, stop acting guilty.

The station is dreary, dreary. Travelers run frantically to escape the rain. Strange: through the window I see them move forward in slow motion. Like the clouds in the sky. Trails of dusk creep into the noisy compartment. Doors slamming. The voices of porters shouting: this way, this way. A frightened child: Mother don't leave me here, I'm afraid. So am I, afraid. Fortunately, the mother finds her child, the porters get their tips, everything turns out all right. It is growing darker, the footsteps are hurried, memories are torn: what must I do to prevent the hallucinations and the prayers and the fears from driving me into madness? I have a vision of our neighbor, the Hasidic Rebbe who is quoting Scriptures: And Moses walked between the living and the dead and the plague ended. His comment: man must learn to separate the living from the dead. Was this why I was on this train? To separate them? And what if that was a mistake? Oh, well, little brother, you know it as well as I do, better than I do: all life is the result of an error.

I am cold. Where on earth is my raincoat? I must

have left it on the bed. I am going to catch my death of
cold. What a joke: I am going to Germany to die of a
cold.

Suddenly, I become apprehensive. I am no longer
cold, I am perspiring. By chance, I am still alone in the
compartment; no need to pretend. Night is falling, it is
still raining; I am afraid of the rain and I am afraid of
night. I am at a crossroad. I have started down an unknown path and at its end a stranger awaits me: I am
Jacob, I am going to fight the angel; one of us shall die.

An image—an old one?—comes to my mind: the white
room—an unpleasant, harrowing white—in the hospital or at the clinic. The soft, appeasing voice of the doctor who tells me not to worry, but I worry. The smile of
a nurse who gently caresses my poor mother's hand to
reassure me, but I am not reassured. The outstretched
hand of a man who tells me not to panic, but I am terrified, I am hallucinating.

I find it difficult to swallow, to breathe. I feel like
screaming but I am dumb; like running but I am paralyzed. I can hear the rustle of wings and madness
around me; yet it is unwarranted: no enemy is lying in
wait for me, I am in no danger. The killer of Davarowsk? I cannot kill him since my father and his crew
have killed him already. What's more, I can leave. Give
up. Nothing prevents me from ending the adventure. I
can get my money back, I am free to get off this train,
change stations, turn back and forget the *Angel* my father has killed, has killed badly. . . . Anyway, my father
is blameless; he hasn't killed anyone; he is innocence
personified. Conclusion: let's stop this foolish game before it goes too far, before the train begins to move.

Only I hesitated too long. No more turning back.
The train is gathering speed.

"I beg your pardon?"

Who is begging my pardon?

"Is this seat reserved?"

In the semidarkness I make out a well-dressed woman; I didn't see her come in.

"No."

She thanks me. Politely I stow away her suitcase, hang up her raincoat; she reiterates her thanks. Now it's my turn to beg pardon—yours, Lisa—for I find the lady traveler attractive. I am partial to grateful women.

"I am going to Graustadt," she says. "And you?"

"Farther."

She seems gentle, attractive and very intelligent, but, please God, let her not be talkative.

"How far is farther?" asks the young woman who may not be as young as all that.

"Farther is very far," I say.

"Am I disturbing you?"

What would she like to hear me say?

"Not at all."

What I should have done is inform her right away that I do not understand French or English or German. A fellow student once did that on a ship bound for the Orient. His table companions were eager to draw him into their games and conversations. Shrugging his shoulders he expressed his regret at not being able to respond for lack of knowledge of their various tongues. Poor wretches: they tried every conceivable method. With no result. My friend was left alone. He meditated, he daydreamed; no one disturbed him. The last evening, as they gathered around the table for a farewell dinner, his companions made one last attempt: "But you communicate, you speak, you say things: what language *do* you use?" "Karaitsu," said he. Of course, there

is no such thing as Karaitsu. My friend had made it up,
just like that; it sounded exotic. But his fellow travelers
were satisfied; they were reassured to find that he did
speak a language, any language, even a nonexistent
one.

"My name is Theresa. And yours?"

"Ariel," I lied.

I could have said Friedman or Béla.

"Ariel," she said. "I like that name."

"So do I."

"And Theresa?"

"I like Theresa."

She laughed. "But you don't know me."

"Yes, I do. Better than you think."

"Impossible. I don't believe you."

"Once upon a time I earned my living telling for-
tunes."

"You read palms?"

"No. I read faces. Those in the field call it 'facial science.' Would you like me to tell you who you are?"

I scowl threateningly as I lean toward her. She is
shaken.

"Then let's not talk," I tell her.

Frightened, she holds her breath. I place my hand on
hers.

"One mustn't be afraid of silence, Theresa. It harms
only those who violate it."

Her hand is warm and welcoming.

In another time, another life, silence was ominous. It
announced the *Angel*. When the ghetto held its breath,
it meant that the military governor was approaching.

He came to shatter the silence, the silence of History before challenging History itself.

And in the clinic, my mother was begging her physician not to abandon her to the white loneliness of her cell: "I am frightened, Doctor, I am frightened of the voiceless voice." He gave her an injection to force her to sleep, to dream as she spoke, to penetrate a world inhabited by other humans, but her fear of the "voiceless voice" haunts me still.

Theresa is smiling at me; she is no longer afraid. Or else: she smiles at me because she likes to be afraid.

She has kept my hand in hers; she is clasping it tightly. If this continues, I'll find myself in another liaison with . . . with whom indeed? Is Theresa German? We had spoken in English; now there is no more need for words. To forget, there is nothing like the awakening of the senses. Sinful? Leave me alone, Simha: go back to your shadows. I am free. Lisa? She'll understand; she who loves them so knows that "trips" are beyond our control. Abdication in the face of His Majesty: chance. Theresa could have taken the next train; I could have stayed behind on the platform. Let's love one another, Theresa; our separation will become that much more symbolic. I feel like telling her this but of course I don't, I don't do anything, I just wait. I listen to the train rushing through a tunnel with a deafening roar and I say nothing.

The image of a dark structure reappears in my mind. The train will arrive, but it will not carry you away, my little brother. Be quiet and listen, says a voice. Listen well, says my mother as she strokes your hair. You will leave us, we have arranged everything, your father and I; we have found some good honest people, you will stay with them; as soon as we can we shall come to take you back; do you hear me? You look at my father in the dark,

he touches your shoulder and presses it hard, he hurts
you but you like it, you would like him to hurt you even
more, you would like him never to remove his hand and
leave it on your shoulder, pressing harder and harder
until your old age. "Come," says my mother. But she
has not spoken; she only thinks she has pronounced the
word: it never passed her lips. Still, you heard it. You
thread your way between the hundred bodies, you are
next to the door. My mother knocks twice, then three
times more slowly; the door half opens, you turn
around, you are looking for your father, you no longer
see him, you no longer see anyone in the dark, besides
you are already outside. A woman grabs you by the
arm: "Here is your mother," your mother tells you;
"whatever you do, don't cry, it's dangerous to cry, it attracts attention: Jewish children cry and that is how
they betray themselves; they cry differently, be careful
my little one, do you promise to be careful?" You promise to promise, but your mother, my mother is no longer
there to receive your promise. The door is closed again.
The night is cold and damp. A dark moonless sky. Inexplicably, you and the woman are backing away
slowly, haltingly. You keep trying to stop but she won't
let you. You are moving away from the building, the
platforms, the empty cars. The early morning mist finds
you in a hut at the edge of the forest. You are sitting
before a bowl of hot milk which you are refusing to
drink. You never saw your mother and father again.
The peasant woman told our parents what happened
after you left them. Your father told me. Since then I
cannot tolerate hot milk.

"First service," the steward yells as he swings his little
bell.

"Are you hungry?"

I shake my head.

"That's suspicious," says she. "A man who does not eat is often hiding something; a man who claims he is not hungry is often a fraud."

"I don't like hot milk," I tell her.

"I understand." Her smile is knowing.

What does she understand? What can she understand? What's the difference; let her think whatever she pleases. I smile back at her, to be polite. And I look her over, wondering whether she could be Lisa or my mother or the peasant woman. She is thirtyish, dark-haired, on the voluptuous side, dressed in an elegant suit and wearing makeup: a woman who does not go unnoticed. Married? Children probably. Strongly believes in women's liberation. Possibly a member of the Red Brigade.

"Where are you going?" the conductor is asking.

"Graustadt," says Theresa.

"And you?"

I hand him my ticket. "Oh, you are going to Reshastadt. You change in Graustadt."

"Yes, I know."

My father. He took the same train once and in his imagination more than a thousand times. I remember his words. Everything seems so familiar that I'm no longer sure whether it is my father or I who is traveling on this train. My head is spinning, I am about to ask Theresa whether she has not made this same journey twenty years ago, whether she has not met a certain Reuven Tamiroff, commentator of Paritus, amateur guardian of justice . . .

"What will you do in Reshastadt?"

"I don't know yet, Theresa."

Theresa: is that her name? Ariel is not mine, and yet
I use it; it protects me from myself. I say "Ariel" and I
become a child again, I relive the child's departure and
then his death.

Theresa: she is neither young nor old, neither beautiful nor ugly, neither clever nor boring, I don't know, I
don't know whether she is woman or mirage.

I only know that we are traveling together, that soon
we are going to go our separate ways. What will she
know of me? She is watching me, that's certain. I feel
her eyes on my body. Too bad. I want nothing. But why
does she persist in spying on me as if I were already her
lover or her enemy?

As always when I try to overcome uneasiness, I focus
my attention on the past. As always I seek refuge in my
parents: will they ever be reunited? I await their return,
their reappearance. . . .

Often at night, as I tried hard to fall asleep, I was
gripped by anxiety: what to do so as not to forget them?
Would I recognize them the following day? She in the
clinic, he in the next room; so far from one another, and
from me. I imagined a small boy swept away by the
crowd; he knows that his father and mother are in there
somewhere yet he passes them by and it is his fault: he
failed to recognize them. "No," he began to sob, "that
will never happen. My mother will speak and I will
know that it is she; my father will touch my shoulder
and I will know that it is he. I shall ask all men to touch
my shoulder and all women to speak to me."

"Are you asleep?"

Barely a whisper. Her lips have not moved. A sleepy
sigh. In German. The familiar "Du" annoys me. I
rationalize: she is dreaming, she is dreaming of someone, she speaks to him in her tongue. That's good, I

need to concentrate. To prepare myself mentally—morally—for the moment when I shall confront the killer of Davarowsk.

The *Angel* and his love of theatrics. His orations, his tricks. His voice demanding silence and that of the crowd reduced to silence. Richard Lander and the end of a world. My parents deported and the death of their son. The death of love and the birth of hate, of the desire for revenge.

I SEE MYSELF standing, awkwardly, before our neighbor Rebbe Zvi-Hersh. I feel clumsy, stupid and for good reason: one does not come to a pious man, a rebbe by profession and a rabbi to boot, saying: "In the name of your teachings, help me: am I right to want to punish an enemy who has massacred our people? Am I right to want to accomplish my father's will? Am I right to want to remain faithful to his oath?" Anyway, that's what I did. The Rebbe received me in his study.

"Yes?" he said, surprised by my visit.

"I am the son of Reuven Tamiroff."

"I know. Simha's friend. Good Jews both of them. Simha . . . is treading on dangerous ground. Kabbalah is the privilege of the initiated."

"I like Simha," I say.

"So do I. But do we like him for the same reasons?"

His eyes and his gaze were like enchanted pools; I had the urge to plunge into them and drown.

"Rebbe," I said, "I'd like to ask you a question. About justice and revenge."

Eyebrows raised, he waited. He had time. He had

two thousand years behind him; they had taught him
the art of waiting.

The Rebbe was watching me. At that moment I realized that he knew more about me and about my father
than I had thought.

"Our God is also the God of vengeance," he replied
after a long moment of reflection. He leaned toward
me, steadying his elbow on a volume of Talmud.
"What does that mean? It means that vengeance is His
domain and His alone."

I could not hold myself back.

"And the assassins of our people? Must they be left
unharmed?"

"I didn't say that. I said the opposite: God will punish them."

"By arranging automobile accidents perhaps?"

"Stop," he said. "Your irony does not offend me. Do
you have faith in divine justice? If not, in what—and in
whom—do you believe?"

"In man."

"In man? What has he done that is so great, so beautiful, so true as to deserve such honor? The assassins,
were they not men as well?"

Confused, I fell silent. The *Angel* committed crimes
against God and against mankind; which are more
damnable? And can they be separated one from the
other?

"Jewish tradition is opposed to capital punishment,"
said the Rebbe in a changed voice. "The Law permits
it, but it behooves us not to implement it. A court that
issues such a verdict is considered murderous. Think: if
a tribunal is encouraged not to enlarge the kingdom of
death, what about an individual? To punish a guilty
man, to punish him with death, means linking yourself
to him forever: is that what you wish?"

"Rebbe," I said.

"Scripture teaches us that it is our duty to kill whoever is preparing to kill us. But does this mean that we are to throw ourselves on just anyone who looks to us like a killer? On the contrary, Torah enjoins us to contemplate this defensive action only if we are certain that the assailant has come with the purpose of killing us. But how is one to acquire such certainty? Supposing that he even states his purpose, how can one be sure that his threats are not meant merely as a deterrent? In other words, the Biblical verse prohibits assassination. It can never be justified."

"Rebbe," I repeated, "listen to me."

"I am listening."

How was I to tell him? I had the feeling he knew why I had come. He was ill-humored. My presence seemed to annoy him.

"I am leaving on a journey," I said. "Wish me success. Give me your blessing."

He rose from his armchair; I also stood up. He stretched his hand toward me but pulled it back immediately.

"No," he said, shaking his head. "I don't want you to leave."

He knew. How did he know? Did he have powers? I didn't think so. And yet . . .

"I have no choice, Rebbe. My soul is at stake. And so is my mind."

"Your soul? Your mind? They have nothing to do with this journey. What you are seeking to resolve *over there,* you can deal with here."

How could I convince him that I had no choice? I was desperate.

"Forgive me, Rebbe. Your refusal to understand hurts me."

My hand reached out to him once more. He looked away.

"I cannot," he said.

And, sinking back into his chair, he reimmersed himself in the study of a question asked two thousand years ago somewhere in Galilee or Yavne, a question of timeless importance.

"I know that you are not asleep," says Theresa.

I jump.

"I knew it," she says triumphantly. "I knew that you were not sleeping."

She knew, she knows; she is proud of it. And here I am, knowing nothing.

"I am thinking about the war," I say.

"War," says Theresa.

Let no one speak to her of war anymore. War is ugly. Nothing but blood, putrefaction, ruins. If only people stopped talking about it, they would stop making it. Intelligent, that Theresa. If mankind were placed in her trust she would make it happy.

"Anyway," she says, "it has nothing to do with me. I was born later."

So was I. And I regret it. What an idea to be born later. If the writings of the Ancients tell the truth, if it is God Himself who decides the destiny of every soul, if it is He Himself who inserts each one individually, carefully, into human time, He has done a poor job with me. Born after the war, I endure its effects. The children of survivors are almost as traumatized as the survivors themselves. I suffer from an Event I have not even experienced. A feeling of void: from a past that has made History tremble I have retained only words. War, for me, is my mother's closed face. War, for me, is my father's weariness.

Of course, I've read countless books on the subject: novels in which everything rings false, essays that are all pretentiousness, films in which facts are embellished and painted and commercialized. None has anything in common with the experience the survivors carry within. War, for me, is Ariel whom I have not known, whom I yearn to know: a false death, a false life, take your choice.

I once asked Simha:

"Why did my father choose the United States?"

"America chose us. Remember the postwar years: no country wanted the survivors. The war was over, we had won it, but we were still treated as though we carried the plague."

"Bontchek went to Palestine."

"Illegally."

"Don't tell me that you are so particular about matters of legality!"

"How can I describe the state we were in? We were tired. Exhausted. To ascend to Palestine, to go on *aliyah*, one needed to be totally committed and have great stamina: one had to cross mountains, rivers, frontiers; one had to walk days and nights, endure hunger and thirst; one had to embark on ships that were not seaworthy, elude the surveillance of the British navy, risk imprisonment in Cyprus: Bontchek was up to it, your parents were not and neither was I."

Still, he is glad that he waited for the American visa,

and so is my father. The American way of life suits them; it is easy to blend in with the masses. Perfect for Simha and my father. Removed, on the sidelines, they pursue their obsessions: Paritus and the savior. New York, the most extroverted city in the world, is also the perfect city for loners. Ideal for madmen. Nobody to disturb them.

"Sometimes your father and I wondered what would have happened if . . ."

". . . if you had gone to Palestine?"

"As many refugees did. We were constantly called upon to go there. We were urged to make our *aliyah;* to live on a kibbutz or in Jerusalem or in Safed in the Galilee: it was tempting."

"If you had gone to Palestine, my father would have finished his book on Paritus and you . . ."

"Me?"

"You would have made the Messiah come out of the shadows."

And I? I would not have roamed through Brooklyn, I would not have lost my mother to that clinic, I would not have met Lisa. . . . The Talmud, with humor, no doubt, attributes to the Creator a secret passion and pastime: He arranges marriages and decisive, meaningful encounters. Lisa's comment: "How is one to explain divorce? Separations? Don't tell me that He too makes mistakes!"

Lisa, what are you doing on this train? Actually, her presence should not surprise me.

"Lisa, you are impossible!"

"Wrong, I'm not impossible, merely improbable."

Surely unpredictable.

She takes everything and gives back more. Lisa equals constant motion. Endless agitation. Pure energy. The need to lose her way, to lose herself. And the celebration of the senses, the madness of desire. She is capable of anything, Lisa is. "Come, let's go for a walk," she'll say at the precise moment when I feel like sleeping or reading. "Let's go to the concert," when I'm having an attack of migraine. "Let's go visit your father," when I'm angry at him and afraid to let it show. "But he is asleep, Lisa." "I'll tell him he is dreaming." He is not asleep. We talk, or rather: Lisa talks, talks: she knows how to charm him, make him laugh; no one has a more beneficial effect on my father; she makes him feel good, that's clear. I believe I love Lisa because my father also loves her. As though following a script, he always says good-bye to her with the same words: "So then, your name is Lisa."

To Lisa, I speak of the war, to Lisa, I speak of all the things that hurt. The war, for her, is my father; and my father, for her, is me.

"People don't understand us, they refuse to understand," says Theresa. "They refuse to take into account our tragedy; they don't stop analyzing that of the others: the Poles, the Ukrainians, the Czechs, the French, the Belgians, the Norwegians, the Freemasons, the priests, the Gypsies and, of course, the Jews, most of all, the Jews, persecuted by us, assassinated by us, by me!"

"You are right, Theresa. People are wrong not to feel as sorry—or even more sorry—for the poor Germans

ELIE WIESEL

who persecuted and massacred the Jews, the priests, the Freemasons . . ."

She doesn't understand or doesn't want to understand my irony; she rattles on:

"All Germans are swine, war criminals, that's all I hear! As soon as the word 'massacre' is pronounced, the German nation comes to mind! As soon as one says 'cruelty' people think of the Germans, of me. . . ."

"You're right, Theresa. It is wrong not to cry over the poor killers, wrong not to pity the poor assassins who exterminated the ghettos, wrong not to be sympathetic to the misfortune of the torturers who reigned over the death camps. It is you who are right, Theresa: the tragedy of the killer is probably greater than that of his victims. The Germans should retaliate against all those who lack consideration for them."

"You are laughing at me," says Theresa, offended.

"Frankly, yes."

"You misunderstood me," she says. "I don't speak of the criminals but of their children. I refer to the young Germans who have done nothing and are hated, judged, despised: their burden is unjust, you must admit!"

There, she was right. I do feel sorry for young Germans because they are tainted, unjustly marked: if they are content it is because they are insensitive; if they are not, it is because they are honest. In other words, in order to be honest they must feel guilty. Isn't that too much to ask of them?

At the university, I avoided the German students. It was as if their language were contaminated, it stood between us like a barbed-wire fence.

"Theresa," I say suddenly, "I am a Jew."

The effect is dramatic. She withdraws into a corner near the window, her face convulsed. She looks at me differently: it is enough to announce to somebody that you are a Jew and he—or she—will look at you differently. Once more she addresses me with the familiar "Du."

"You are a Jew, a Jew. You are Jewish, Jewish."

The situation becomes comical. Theresa, moved by who knows what kind of impulse, a desire to make up for past grievances perhaps, leaves her seat and comes to sit next to me. She takes both my hands in her own and squeezes them violently while whispering incoherent sentences. I catch two words: *Liebchen* and *Angst*. What is the connection? Is she studying philosophy? She may be trying to reassure me that her *Liebchen* of the moment need endure no *Angst*. Except that *Angst* is something of which I have plenty: there is a knot in my stomach while I travel on German soil. I am going to confront a man I have met only through his victims' eyes. Theresa senses my discomfort, she offers me her help, her compassion, her passion. I feel her pulse quickening. I'd like to withdraw my hands but I don't, it is as though I am detached from her, I leave her to her adventures, I think of something else, I swear to myself never to forget, never to forgive. . . .

"Why do you refuse to understand *our* tragedy?" says Theresa, who is beginning to look tired.

I swear to myself to try to understand all tragedies, hers included; even if, of course, it has nothing to do with that of the Jews.

Thank God, she's asleep. The single bulb's bluish light bounces off her throat and slides down her chest. What or whom is she dreaming of? I dream of Lisa. In my delirium I see her at the mercy of the *Angel*. I am angry with my father and Simha: their failure has a meaning and I don't know what it is. Perhaps simply this: that the killer is stronger than his victims. The

Angel, all alone, has assassinated thousands and thousands of Jews, but all the Jews of the world are powerless against him. Could the killers be immortal? I see myself, in the living room, showing the photograph to my father and Simha. The distraught face of one, the incredulity of the other. The weeks of rest in the mountains, at the seashore, wiped away, vanished. I was in such a rush to make the plane, I even forgot my raincoat. What else did I forget? The night flight, the day in Frankfurt: I am yearning for sleep. To sleep. For good. Like in the sealed cars, long ago. That would be stupid. Theresa would discover my corpse. Her cry of horror. Paritus, my friend, is it you who said: "Every cry is a cry for help?" Paritus, you're an old fool.

I am cold. A vague sensation of imminent defeat; the sudden feeling of being the bearer of bad luck. A desire to join my mother in her clinic. Through the mist I observe the ghosts moving about slowly; some are veiled, others can be seen only from the back. Are they talking? I hear nothing. Yet I *know* what they are saying. An old man wanders back and forth as if seeking someone: an enemy, a brother? Inexplicably he begins to laugh. A woman numb with cold seems ready to explode with anger. The train is rocking me but not enough to make me fall asleep.

Theresa moves restlessly; she is nervous because I am nervous. In her dreams she tries perhaps to understand me. She sleeps and I watch her sleep. And I think of Lisa: I like to watch her sleep. The better to possess her? The better to give myself to her. And deep inside me there is a small frightened Jewish boy who looks at her with me, through me, a small boy killed by a highborn German officer.

Sleep, Theresa. Surely I am not angry with you. The only being who really inspires animosity, a fierce ha-

tred, in me is the *Angel.* The others don't count. He
alone obsesses me. I want to hate him, I hate him for
having killed and for having escaped death. Everything
inside me demands that my hate grow from day to day,
from memory to memory, from page to page. It is because I cannot hate anyone that I am determined to
hate him. It is because I am against violence that I wish
for his defeat, his agony. Even though I cannot hurt
anyone, I want to imagine, I want to see him dead, to
complete my father's work, to finally taste revenge. Af-
terward, I shall stand before my father and tell him: "I
have seen the man responsible for Ariel's death, I have
seen the assassin of the Jews of Davarowsk." And he
will say: "All right, so you've seen him; what have you
done with him?" That is the question. What am I going
to do, my God, what am I going to do?

Did I doze off? Suddenly, it's dawn; the sun's rays fil-
ter into the compartment. The train speeds along,
growling and groaning, like a sick animal fleeing
through the night.

Theresa opens one eye, seems surprised to discover
me next to her, then remembers. She stretches smiling.

"We're arriving soon."

She stands up, straightens her skirt, her blouse, her
hair; I look away.

"Half an hour," she says.

She takes her handbag, goes to the lavatory and
comes back combed, made up, buttoned, her face under
control. Who is she? Theresa, a common name. Theresa
who? What kind of life does she lead? The next minutes
are both long and fleeting and, in any case, unnerving.
Whatever I say will ring false. Polite banalities. And
what if I grabbed her, just like that, without preamble?
Not my style. And then she'd say: really, you Jews. . . .

And also: Lisa would be upset with me. And my father. What's more, I don't feel like it. A word of advice from our dear Paritus comes to mind: "To journey through life, man must choose between nausea and a smile."

"I hope that your visit to Germany will be successful and pleasant," says Theresa.

Successful and pleasant? Precisely the words she should not have used. The *Angel* used them before sending the Jews of Davarowsk to be "relocated." If he wished them a successful journey, it meant that he had marked them for annihilation; if he predicted for them a pleasant journey, it meant that he was sending them to a hard labor camp.

"You are the first Jew I have met," says Theresa. "You're not as I imagined them. You encourage and reject with the same gesture. You'd like to inspire affection but you're too scared. You run away from the present and reach simultaneously into the future and into the past so that in the end you are nowhere."

I pretend not to smile, to understand, to consent, I pretend that I am evolving outside the present, beyond time; I pretend to be engaged in living.

At last, the train slows down. Here are the sidings, the platforms of Graustadt's central station. Theresa moves toward the door; a moment's hesitation: should she kiss me? Take me as lover, confidant, yoga instructor? She settles for a shrug of the shoulders and a goodbye of the most ordinary kind.

I step off the train. I have two or three hours to waste waiting for the connection. The outrageously modern station is a gigantic supermarket where travelers can buy anything: a woman for the morning, insurance with a suicide clause or a lifetime ticket on the German Railroad System.

Between nausea and a smile, what does one choose?

Dᴵᴰ I ʟᴇᴀᴠᴇ the station? Did I hallucinate? I have the feeling of making another "trip," this time without Lisa, to the other side. I am and I am not myself. Aimlessly I roam through Graustadt and yet I know that I am expected here. In a narrow alley, near a large square bordered by a park, I notice two women—a mother who vaguely resembles mine and a daughter who reminds me of Lisa—they are standing in front of a dilapidated building, they are crying.

"Please don't," I tell them. "You mustn't cry. It's dangerous. Tears attract attention. Do you want to be arrested? Do you want to die?"

They pretend not to hear or not to understand what I am telling them; but it could also be that I did not say this but something else or even nothing at all.

"Come in," says the mother. "You did well to come," she adds blowing her nose.

"I knew that you would come," says the daughter. "You were his friend."

"Your father had many friends," corrects her mother. "Look at them, here they come. How nice of them."

Indeed, men and women are converging on them, all

of a certain age, well dressed but colorless. They greet the two women and disappear inside the building.

"Please come in," says the mother. "Follow us. We shall begin."

I observe her winking at her daughter who winks back. Oh well, that's their problem. I push open the door and enter what looks like a packed funeral parlor. Someone pushes me toward a chair, I sit down: I need it badly, my legs are hurting.

"Ladies and gentlemen," says a man who resembles Lenin but pretends to be a priest, "on behalf of our dear Ludwig Semmel's family, I thank you for having come in such great numbers. Ludwig was our brother, our irreplaceable benefactor. Our loss is great and our pain is immense."

"He speaks well," whispers an old lady, nudging her ailing husband. "I hope he'll be available when your turn comes."

"Exemplary father, faithful husband, devoted friend, Ludwig deserved the admiration we felt for him," continues the priest Lenin. "He was a saint, nay, more than a saint: an angel."

He expresses himself in flowery, mawkish language. The audience is ecstatic, mesmerized; some people make a move as if to applaud but think better of it.

"Never, do you hear me, never shall we forget him," the priest is spouting, "never shall we forget Ludwig Semmel, the man who . . ."

Overwhelmed by emotion, he withdraws from the podium and returns to his seat in the first row. The two women break out their handkerchiefs, followed by the rest of the audience, with the exception of those who do not own one and who make do with the backs of their hands.

The next speaker is a bald man who stutters:

"I miss Lud-d-wig and you-you . . ."

Here and there I hear noises of irritation; when one is a stutterer one does not make speeches. But the speaker has his own reasons that no one can contest: the deceased and he were business associates. Therefore the survivor must proclaim the truth: contrary to local gossip, L-Lud-dwig had been an honest man. Ev-ven if-if one crossed the p-planet, one could never find a more honest associate. . . .

Others echo him. Philanthropist, patron of the arts, protector of widows, Ludwig Semmel shall have his statue. Ludwig Semmel, Ludwig Semmel: who is he? Have I met him? I am searching my memory when I become aware of the fact that all eyes are fixed on me.

"Your turn," says the widow.

"Speak," says the daughter.

I should answer that they are mad, that I have never had the honor of meeting their father and husband, that I am a Jew from Brooklyn who has never spoken in public for the excellent reason that nobody ever asked me to, but they are all staring at me so insistently that I hesitate to refuse. As in a dream I see myself rising to my feet and walking toward the pulpit, I see and hear myself deliver an incoherent speech in which I compare Cicero and Paritus, Schiller and John Donne whose eulogy I finally deliver: the daughter seems delighted; her softly shining eyes gaze at me intently. As for the mother, she waits until I finish to take her turn at the pulpit:

"The last speaker is the only man my deceased husband considered a true friend. The others are liars, cheats. Holtz, do you think I have forgotten the matter of the fake jewels? And you Fleischmann, do you think my husband didn't know that you tried to seduce our daughter?"

The widow was in top form. She elicits the response you can imagine. Timidly at first, and then more noisily, people begin to protest and show their displeasure. As for the widow, she is not to be intimidated: it is the greatest settling of accounts I have ever witnessed. Three women faint, two men run away. Aloof, uninvolved, I watch the scene: I await my awakening to understand.

"Who are you?" the widow is demanding to know.

"Yes, where are you from?" the daughter asks.

"My name is Ariel."

"You are a liar," they shout hysterically.

"My name is Ariel. Ariel, Ariel!"

"Lies! You're lying, he's lying! He is making fun of us! He has come with the sole purpose of making fun of us, of ridiculing our plight, of imposing guilt on our people!"

"My name is Ariel and I am a Jew, I come from Brooklyn and Davarowsk, from Wizhnitz and Lodz, from Debrecen and from Bendzin . . ."

The women who have fainted come to, the fugitive men reappear to join the mob; if I escaped death it is because, despite what you may think, miracles did not cease with Moses and Joshua.

T HE *Angel* and I were alone; one always is with Death. Enshrined behind his immaculate desk, he was eyeing me in an arrogant, polite and curiously detached way. Armed, I could have gunned him down. At one particular moment, just before the end, in the instant of recognition, I was standing so close to him I could have strangled him. I was free, I had the luxury of weighing all the options, of eliminating all extraneous motives. I had the leisure to consider the act before acting. And to correct a page of History, if not History itself.

Free? A hasty word, used incorrectly. The act that commits a person sums him up in his entirety, for it commits everybody. Paritus was not wrong in his attack on Homer: the weight of the past is heavier than that of the future. Death negates the future tense but not the years, the hours that have elapsed. My ancestors are present for me within my endeavor; my decision binds them, for through me they are able to act. On that level, individual freedom, albeit unlimited, seems inconceivable.

And therefore I don't know whether my inaction should elicit regret or the opposite of regret from me.

Cowardice or courage? The fact remains that, at the last moment, the so-called moment of truth, I sidestepped the decision. The act contemplated by my father has met with failure once again. I know that I should apologize, beg to be pardoned; I feel guilty. Guilty for having confronted the enemy without defeating him.

And yet it was easy. . . .

With the help of details gleaned from my father, I quickly find my bearings in this small provincial town. My father is with me as I follow the Birnbaum Allee until I reach the Kaiser Friedrich Platz. He is still at my side as I discover the changes that have taken place in Reshastadt. No more rubble, no more ruins. Suspicion, mistrust and superficial politeness have given way to enjoyment, courtesy and consumption. In one generation, the vanquished have succeeded in erasing the visible traces of their defeat.

A few bank notes, a few lies and a few compliments and the trick is played. As an "American journalist on assignment," I'm given the best room in the Hotel Italien, access to the local daily's archives and the cooperation of the public relations office of the Elektronische Laboratorien TSI whose chief executive is Herr Wolfgang Berger.

His secretary is pretty, provocative, efficient. As in fiction, she admires her boss. As in the movies, she protects him. Her smile is cool, her demeanor firm.

"The Herr Direktor is on the telephone, he will receive you momentarily. May I bring you something to drink?"

She is hospitable, helpful: she will do all she can to see that her boss will make the best possible impression

on me. I wonder how far she would go to ensure favor-
able press coverage. I wonder how far she would go to
conquer me?

The door on the left opens, a man appears and invites me to come in. The office is spacious, elegant,
filled with light. No superfluous object. Perfect taste.
You can see: Wolfgang Berger is a man of culture.

"Please sit down. I am told that you have just arrived. I hope that, thanks to you, our city will become
famous. It deserves it, believe me."

"Of course I believe you."

To break the ice he launches into a monologue on the
responsibilities and abuses of the press.

"You are right," I tell him. "Sometimes journalists
have nothing to say so they say anything at all."

"Not you."

"Oh, well, I'm neither better nor worse than my colleagues."

He protests smiling. I watch him intensely.

"What do you think of the German nation?"

"I beg your pardon?"

I have not understood his question. He repeats it.

"The German nation, the German nation," I say
while forcing myself to think logically and coherently
enough not to appear suspect in his eyes. "To which
German nation are we referring: yesterday's or today's?
The hate that prevails in this divided country reminds
me of another, a thousand times bloodier, except that
today's is also directed inward: the fanatic militants,
the bloodthirsty extremists, the preachers of destruction, the Black and Red Brigades of arbitrary death.
Your generation hated the Jews; now your youth in
turn repudiates you, their elders. Not for the sake of the
Jews, of course, but for the sake of authority. Such are
the dynamics of hate: it overflows. One begins by hat-

ing a social group and one ends up despising society; one begins by persecuting the Jews and one ends up threatening mankind. All hate becomes self-hate."

Herr Direktor Wolfgang Berger listens attentively; his hands clasped before him on the table he concentrates his energy in his eyes. When he decides to ask me a question, his voice is nasal and unsure:

"Why are you so preoccupied with hate, sir? What I mean is: why do you approach it with such passion?"

I study him and, curiously, I have a clearer vision of the objects surrounding us; I even notice the paintings on the wall behind me. I glimpse a fly on the ceiling.

"I am Jewish, Herr Direktor."

"I know. I knew it from the first moment."

Only natural, I tell myself. He possesses great experience in the matter; he knows how to recognize a Jew. Like a well digger smells water, he smells Jews. In their presence his killer instinct awakens.

"Would you permit me a question?"

I nod.

"Is it because you're Jewish that you hate me? Do you hate all Germans?"

Asked in a neutral, almost scientific tone, his questions trouble me. Does he suspect my identity? A mad thought races through my mind: I resemble my brother. Nonsense. The explanation is much simpler: the killer in him has recognized me as a victim.

"No, Herr Direktor. I feel no animosity toward the German people; I don't believe in collective guilt. I belong to a people that has suffered its consequences too long to ever apply it to others. I shall go one step, six million steps, further and tell you that even the executioner does not inspire hate in me: it would be too foolish to reduce an ontological Event to a word, a gesture, an impulse of hate."

"But then, dear sir, what are you seeking in Germany?"

I feel like answering him: one man, one man alone, one killer has motivated my journey; one malevolent being, an ally of Evil, it behooves me, in the name of my flesh and blood, to remove from life, for there ought not to be room on the planet earth for him and us. Too soon. Should I answer directly that I came to Germany out of a sense of justice that has nothing to do with hate?

"I know that your time is precious . . ."

I almost said limited; I caught myself.

". . . but, with your permission, I should like to tell you a story."

He flinches: he must have made some connection. No doubt he mentally calculated my age, the years elapsed since the war, the various possibilities. . . . His nostrils quiver. His posture stiffens perceptibly.

"I am at your disposal," he says amiably.

"It's a story of suffering and war," I say.

"I like stories but I detest wars."

"It's a story of Jewish suffering and it takes place during the war against the Jews. In a ghetto somewhere in Central Europe. . . ."

His pupils have changed color; the fly changes position on the ceiling.

"Yes," says he.

Now he knows that I know. The beast tensed on his haunches, waits. I sense the danger. I rise, I sit down again. I act without a plan, I improvise.

"In a ghetto somewhere," he says with the same nasal inflection. "Please go on."

I call upon all those whose destinies have fashioned mine. I mobilize all my resources of energy, imagination and memory to give each sentence, each pause, the intensity and fire of authenticity. I speak and I am transported elsewhere. I speak and I know that it is to speak here to this man, that I have lived through more than one life, accepted so many challenges and deciphered so many symbols.

I describe the ghetto of Davarowsk: its famished children, its talented beggars, its fallen princes. In the early morning hours a man leaves his family and goes to work; he never returns. At night, a mother discovers her five sons: shot down in the woods. A couple lives locked in an airless room and dies of suffocation. Vignettes of misery, fragments of despair: I could multiply them to infinity.

"Go on," says Wolfgang Berger.

I go on. The sessions of the Jewish Council. The deportations. The "actions." Death? There was worse; there was the humiliation that preceded death. There was the executioner who meant to have his victims crawl at his feet before he slaughtered them or sent them to be exterminated. There was the killer who demanded that his victims listen to him with admiration and worship him as a God. There were the prayers that the Jews refused to recite upon command, there was the soldiers' sneering, the death rattle of old men sprawling in their blood, there were the mass graves where the corpses lay piled into high mountains, their shifting summits reaching into the dark and menacing clouds.

There were so many events, so many mutilated, buried destinies, that I could spend my life and that of my people evoking them. Even if all the Jews in the world were to do nothing but testify, we would not succeed in filling more than one page. However, the Book contains six million pages.

As I speak, the lines of his face grow sharper and

deeper; he is turning paler and paler minute by minute, episode by episode. He is afraid, oh, yes, the *Angel* of fear is dominated by fear, transfixed by fear; Death has finally caught up with the *Angel* of Death. Briefly, I feel vindicated: bravo Ariel! So you are capable of inspiring, of inflicting terror! Are you satisfied, Ariel? Are you proud of what I've achieved?

"I have not finished," I tell him.

I am filled with dazzling insight: the words come to me easily as though they were seeking me.

"One more story. Just one. The last. It is about a Jewish child, five or six years old. You knew him; you also knew his father. Reuven and Ariel Tamiroff, do those names mean anything to you?"

I tell him the story of my little brother. The *Angel* had noticed my father and mother at the station. The cattle cars were there waiting next to the platforms. The Germans had completed their count of those leaving when the military governor issued a brief order: "Wait!" Barely able to conceal his resentment, he came closer to confront my parents: "You have a son, where is he?" My father did not reply. The *Angel* slapped him: "Where is your son?" My father bit his lips and said nothing. Then my mother came to his aid: "Our son is dead, sir. Carried away by a terrible fever, our son left us two months ago. Ask the people, they will confirm it." "I don't believe you," shouts the military governor. "She is telling the truth," says a voice from behind my parents. "Who are you?" "My name is Simha Zeligson. I have known the Tamiroff family for years. I buried the maternal grandparents, the paternal grandparents; I also buried the son. I swear it on my life." Other voices join his. The military governor is not satisfied; he dispatches a group of SS to the ghetto: "If you have to turn it upside down, bring back the little

Tamiroff!" The SS searched the ghetto from one end to the other and came back empty-handed. "Never mind," said the *Angel* to my parents. "I shall catch your little boy, I promise you; you won't be here anymore to see it and that I regret." He kept his word. He initiated an elaborate manhunt and ultimately succeeded in tracking down my little brother. His vengeance was terrible and cruel, people spoke of it in all the ghettos near and far.

"I shall not ask you *why* you committed all these crimes," I said to him. "I shall ask you only *how* you could commit them. *How* you could be present at so many executions, decree so much torture without giving up your sleep, your mind, your taste for lovemaking and wine, your memory? *How* could you inflict such suffering without it leaving its mark on your face? *How* could you perpetrate death and not endure it? You were Death, how did you succeed in staying alive?"

My head touched his, almost. To avoid mingling our breaths, I moved back a centimeter.

"Ariel Tamiroff, do you remember Ariel Tamiroff, sir? You made him endure a slow death in front of the ghetto's last Jews as they stood under a frozen sky: *how* could you inflict such pain on a small boy whom a thousand mouths were silently blessing, hoping to make him into their messenger in heaven?"

Had he answered, I would have killed him. A killer's life is as fragile as his victim's. One move and Wolfgang Berger was finished. Nothing would have been easier. End of the *Angel*. Any answer, any attempt at self-justification and I would have committed the irreparable. But he merely frowned and narrowed his eyes, focusing on me as if to better place me. The silent confrontation lasted but one second. I glanced at my watch: two hours had elapsed since I appeared in his office. Any moment now, his secretary would knock at the door to announce another visitor, or the office closing hour or the end of the world.

And now? In just two hours I had crossed centuries of horrors; the journey had exhausted me.

"Who are you?"

His question was an arrow. Should I inform him that I was his judge and he my prisoner?

"Who are you, sir?" he asked again, his voice harsh and tense. "I demand an answer!"

He spoke easily, all trace of fear gone from his face. His choice of words, his slow and heavy delivery, the icy inflection of his voice made me shiver: was this how he addressed my little brother and my father?

"Who am I? My name is Ariel."

I paused and then:

"Like my little brother; I am named Ariel for my brother. I am a child. A child of the ghetto of Davarowsk. Every Jew of the ghetto was my parent. Every wall imprisons me, every lie betrays me."

Another pause.

"And every dead victim is my brother."

He ran his tongue over his parched lips; he was having difficulty breathing. Yet, he appeared neither defeated nor chastened.

"What do you plan to do?"

I had not really given it any thought.

"Hand me over to the police? Denounce me in the press?"

In my thoughts I summon my father and his friend Simha, my sick mother and my friend Bontchek to help me, advise me. An old saying crosses my mind: "The Lord may wish to chastise, that is His prerogative; but it is mine to refuse to be His whip." Where had I picked that up? From my father? From Rebbe Zvi-Hersh, our neighbor? I saw myself with the Rebbe during our conversation about vengeance. Abruptly I realized that the individual sitting across from me no longer held any real interest for me. Once the words had been exchanged, I could leave. The *Angel* no longer provoked in me either hatred or thirst for revenge. I had disturbed the pattern of his existence, renewed his memory, spoiled his future joys, that was enough for me. He could no longer act, live, laugh as though he had never used the ghetto of Davarowsk as his stage and his universe.

I shall speak. I shall tell the tale. The *Angel* must be, will be, unmasked. I shall describe the solitude of the survivors, the anguish of their children. I shall relate the death of my little brother. I shall set forth, I shall recall the wounds, the moanings, the tears. I shall speak of the voices of dusk, the mute violence of night. I shall recite the *Kaddish* of dawn. The rest is no longer within my scope.

And my father? Will he be angry with me? And Simha, will he take offense? I don't think so. Neither one looks upon the act of murder as an answer. Wittingly or unwittingly, they had done what was right. Their failure must be viewed within a larger context. Nor should it embarrass them or shame them. Justice must be human, it passes through language which must be justified by memory. Only in life are just words translated into acts of justice; never in death.

"You will never know peace," I say as I get to my feet.

My head afire, I am no longer certain that I said it. I am no longer certain that I stood up. This encounter, this confrontation, could I have lived them in a dream?

"Wherever you are you shall feel like an intruder pursued by the dead," I say. "Men will think of you with revulsion; they will curse you like the plague and war; they will curse you when they curse Death."

Like my brother before me, I leave moving backward. For fear that he may shoot me in the back? That he may pierce me with a poisoned dagger? I detect his aborted motions, his somber glances, his thoughts, I search them, I rummage through them, through him, I track them down, I weigh them, I examine them: is there an evil thought, a diabolical thought in that head? What trick is he about to play on me? What must I do to avoid the trap, what means must I seize to save my little brother? Fever has gripped my whole body, I know that I am living the gravest moment of my life and perhaps even of my brother's life and yet I know that all this may be nothing but a dream, a demented hallucination; I see myself breathing and choking, I observe myself sitting and standing, victor and victim, living and dead, I see myself walking backward as I look upon the *Angel*, as I stare at him saying to myself over and over: he must look at me as long as possible. I am already at the door, my hand grips the knob, I feel my heart pounding and at the same time I feel a great calm come over me and I can hear myself saying slowly, very slowly:

"You wanted to know who I am, I shall tell you: I am a Jewish child named Ariel and you are my prisoner; you are the prisoner of Davarowsk Ghetto, the prisoner of the dead Jews of the ghetto of Davarowsk."

The last image I take away of him surprises me nevertheless; I realize that the *Angel* is, after all, different from most human beings: one day I shall know in what way.

IT IS 1984 when I reread these writings, some of which go back twenty years and others ten. Times have changed. And I? I—who?

Until today I maintain complex relations with my name. Ariel Tamiroff designates another than myself: a small Jewish boy, son of Rachel and Reuven Tamiroff of Davarowsk, whom History's violence carried away in a storm of ashes. I had observed in myself a gradual splitting into two: Ariel was and was not dead; I was and was not alive. Ariel lived inside me, through me; I talked to him to convince myself of his existence; I listened to him to persuade myself of mine. At first, it was: He, Ariel. Then: You, Ariel. And finally: I, Ariel.

Were Ariel alive, he would be forty-six years old; he would be a father, a professor of literature or philosophy, a liberal, a humanist. I am thirty-five years old. Lisa has left me; I miss her.

My father will soon complete his definitive commentary on the *Meditations* of his dear Paritus; my mother is no longer at the clinic, she died shortly after my return from Germany. We were not at her bedside, Simha was. He told us that one hour before she died, she regained all her faculties: she asked him questions about us, about what was happening in the world, about the physicians taking care of her. She died in the middle of a question regarding my relationship with Lisa. Strange: she never mentioned Ariel.

Simha has aged; he has not yet hastened the coming of the Messiah, but he will surely succeed; I believe in him. His calculations of the mystical *Gematria* have been erroneous till now but that does not mean he should abandon them. Besides, he has no intention of doing so, no more than he has any intention of closing down his business. He continues to buy and sell shadows; I think he manages quite well.

And so does Bontchek, thank you. From the time my father began treating him as Simha's equal, he has been content, sometimes even happy, with or without his slivovitz.

As for myself, I teach in a small university in Connecticut. I love my students and feel hurt when they don't reciprocate my love.

Since my journey to Reshastadt I have visited many countries as—you will laugh—correspondent for a weekly newsmagazine. I have been sent—on assignments of varying lengths—to France, India and Israel. Though I am a Jew of the Diaspora, I am attached to Israel with every fiber of my being. Jerusalem is the only place where I feel at home. May I quote Agnon? "Like every Jew, I was born in Jerusalem but the Romans invaded my city and pushed my cradle all the way to Galicia."

I have made a conscious effort not to forget; subconsciously, I have tried no less to forget. An Oriental sage made me see this one day: "As you articulate one word, you suppress another; as you evoke one image, you must repress another. This is true also of memories: to remember certain events, you must forget certain others." Often I fail, they are too tangled.

Still, it's no good deceiving myself, I look upon my life not as a failure but as a defeat. Son of survivors, I feel ill at ease in a complacent world that, in order to rest easier, has repudiated me even before my birth. For me all is constraint: language and silence, love and the absence of love. What I wish to say, I shall never say. What I wish to understand, I shall never understand.

The era we are now living through brings us closer to the catastrophe foreseen by Orwell, the prophet, not the writer. What he predicted would happen, has already happened. We live outside ourselves, beside ourselves. To paraphrase a noted philosopher: my contemporaries create small circumstances out of great events. What will the year 2000 be made of? Like Simha, I see shadows lifting the horizon; from afar I glimpse the immense shadow, not unlike a monstrous, poisonous mushroom, linking heaven and earth to condemn and destroy them. Could this be the ultimate punishment? Simha, the kabbalist, claims that after the punishment will come redemption. But of what kind? A Hasidic Master sees with greater accuracy: the Messiah may well come too late; he will come when there will be no one left to save. Never mind, I shall wait nonetheless.

I have been waiting for years, for centuries. I have waited to rediscover my father. I have waited to meet my brother. I have attempted to live their lives by assuming them as my own. I have said "I" in their stead. Alternately, I have been one or the other. Surely we have had our differences, our quarrels, our conflicts; but the differences have been transformed into renewed ties. Now, more than ever, my love for my father is whole as though he were my son and as though I were his, the one he lost over there, far away.

A sad summing up: I have moved heaven and earth, I have risked damnation and madness by interrogating the memory of the living and the dreams of the dead in order to live the life of those who, near and far, continue to haunt me: but when, yes when, shall I finally begin to live my life, my own?

ABOUT THE AUTHOR

Elie Wiesel is the recipient of numerous distinguished literary awards, including *Le Grand Prix de la Littérature de la Ville de Paris* for his most recent novel, *The Fifth Son*; and *Le Prix Livre-Inter* for his novel *The Testament*. In 1984 he received the U.S. Congressional Gold Medal and was named a Commander of the French Legion of Honor. Mr. Wiesel is University Professor and Andrew Mellon Professor in the Humanities at Boston University, and chairman of the United States Holocaust Memorial Council. He and his family live in New York City, where his annual lectures at the 92nd Street Y have drawn standing room only audiences for nearly two decades.